"Fool," said my Muse to me, "look in thy heart and write."

STATE of
INDEPENDENCE

Robert Farrar

First published in 1993 by GMP Publishers Ltd
P O Box 247, London N17 9QR, England

World Copyright © 1993 Robert Farrar

A CIP catalogue record for this book
is available from the British Library

ISBN 0 85449 194 5

Distributed in North America by InBook
P O Box 120470, East Haven, CT 06512, USA

Distributed in Australia by Bulldog Books
P O Box 155, Broadway, NSW 2007, Australia

Printed and bound in the EC on environmentally-friendly paper
by Nørhaven A/S, Viborg, Denmark

To all true seekers of the Light.
May what they find herein sustain them
in their search for the Quintessence;
the Stone of the Philosophers, true Wisdom
and perfect Happiness, the *Summum Bonum*.

Thanks to Ian for the word-processor
and to Jules for the photocopying.

Part One

DECLARATIONS OF INDEPENDENCE

ONE

The story of how I lost that which can never be regained — my innocence — has amused many a dinner party of bright young same-sexers in the Hammersmith and Shepherds Bush neck of the woods. My flatmate Eric says it is the most erotic story he has ever heard — which is good of him, really, considering it was his lovely boyfriend Corey who seduced me. Eric says he's going to write it up one day, whop in a few tiny but crucial alterations, and sell it to a women's magazine for £150. *Bella*, perhaps, or *Me*. I tell him, Eric, that story will never be suitable for a women's magazine, no matter how many alterations you put in. You can make one of us a girlie if you like, you can chop out all the religion business, but it'll still be too hot to handle. Because that's the type of story it is. But Eric is Adam Ant. That story is worth the princely sum of £150, he says, spooning exactly six spoonfuls of sugar into his tea, and that is exactly what it is going to earn us.

The truth is, we have even worked out exactly how we are going to spend the £150:

Two pairs of fabulous never-wear-out Doctor Martens
Therapeutic Air-Cushion-Sole Boots:
 @ £40 each £80.00
Two return coach fares to Brighton:
 @ £13.99 each £27.98
Two luxury Marks and Spencer picnic lunches:
 @ £5 each (approx) £10.00
One bottle drinkable red wine: £3.99
Two slap-up pizza dinners at the Duomo restaurant
(where what you want is not on the menu, as they say)
 @ £8.50 each £17.00
Beer budget (£5 each) £10.00
Contingency .... £ 1.03

GRAND TOTAL £150.00

   This careful breakdown of the £150 we are going to make when the story of my fall from grace is one day transformed, as if by magic, into fodder consistent with the tastes of a million exploited home-makers has been carefully typed out and stuck onto the inside of the door of the cupboard wherein we keep our herb teas and caffeine-free cereal-based "health" drinks and a small tupperware pot of hazelnuts which has been there for some time and which is now infested with horrible little winged insects. Our Swedish flatmate Bjorn has pointed out to us, in his infinite wisdom, that the presence of this pot of hellish hazelnuts is *unhigurnic*, but unfortunately such problems are bound to arise when more than three people live together under one roof. No one knows who the hazelnuts belong to. Therefore no one can ever throw them away. We could only throw them away if we could have a meeting at which every member of the household was present, and so far this elegant method of solving the problem, though often proposed and universally endorsed, has never been pulled off. Actually no one is entirely sure who is living in the house.

   From time to time we take down the piece of paper with the plan for spending the £150 on it and make a little alteration to the sums — a £2 cutback on the beer budget, perhaps, in order to allow for a more extravagant pizza dinner; the impulsive all-out axing of the Marks and Spencer lunch in favour of a quick heads-round-the-door visit to that marvellous basement disco just down the road from the Pier: little alterations like this. The basic thrust of the thing, however, has remained unchanged ever since it has been stuck there, which by now must be well over a year. Time flies! It seems like only yesterday that I moved in with Eric and Tookie and all the rest of them, but I think we are talking years here, if the truth be told. For let us not forget that I was but a fresh young chicken of nineteen summers that fateful day when Eric's lovely boyfriend Corey broke the ice in ways for which my sheltered provincial upbringing had left me quite unprepared.

I remember, after being exhaustively ravished, lying spent and husk-like on a second-hand leopard-skin-pattern sofa which was in the house at the time and bleating something about having lost my faith. I'm not entirely sure, but I believe Corey replied with a sharp, dismissive little laugh — and quite right too, of course. My whole God-phase was obviously no more than the only partially sublimated sexual energy of a teenage swot whose healthy appetite for male flesh had been thwarted and starved at every turn by a monotonous succession of patriarchs.

I was brought up on the South Coast, you see, far from the liberating cosmopolitanism of Hammersmith and Shepherds Bush, and further still from those marvellous wide-open spaces which I've heard you get to the north of the country, where long walks over hills and dales loosen the limbs and surely make rare that particular condition of bloodless self-satisfaction in which my family was steeped. By the age of sixteen I had completed what my teachers had been so fun-loving as to term an education, and it was to take me three long years to persuade my father to allow me to take a job in the capital city, whither I was lured by forces I only dimly understood. During this time I toyed with a career as a librarian, and the intolerable tedium of my life was only briefly interrupted once a year by summer holidays of a religious nature, which consisted of me being bundled off to an old hunting lodge in Dorset where my time was to be equally divided between contemplation of the Holy Scripture and canoeing down rivers with my excruciatingly incorruptible chums. Don't ask. Don't ask. We were each assigned an older boy at the beginning of the holiday who we were told was our "father" ("father" indeed!), and whose job it would be to accompany us on our canoeing trips and also to banter with his "son", during mellow rural moments, upon sacred themes. The last "father" I had was marvellously high-classed, an Etonian I think, called Nicky, with lovely nut-coloured hair and khaki shorts. My faith, like a small frightened animal, trembled within me, sensing that its doom was assured.

Upon my nineteenth birthday I persuaded my bloodless father to allow me to take on an exciting clerical job in Hammersmith which, in terms of salary and prospects, constituted no less than a quantum leap from my librarian career, which frankly hadn't really taken off. My father, who had just watched John Travolta and Olivia Newton-John in *Grease* on the TV, and who had been convinced by his viewing of this somewhat anodyne *divertissement* that the Devil was at loose in the world, was, at first, Adam Ant: no child of his would be found within four square miles of Cleopatra's Needle after sundown. My mother, however, for whom the pleasure of cooking my meals and washing my clothes had palled a little over the past nineteen years, took my side in this, and at last I was given permission to leave. Arrangements were made for me to stay with an aunt in Chiswick and to spend most of my time outside work hours going from door to door trying to make converts for the somewhat overzealous church to which she belonged. It was a start.

You probably don't want to know all this but it's sort of important to the story of how I came to lose that which can never be regained. How Eric thinks he can reduce the thing to 1,500 words (which is the length that a story has to be if you are going to sell it to a woman's magazine for £150 — I think the idea is you get 10p a word) I really do not know. He says the whole religion thing will have to go, and I can see that would make the story shorter, but I feel very strongly that if you do this you end up with no story at all. Eric is always on the look-out for cunning scams. He is of the opinion that it is worth spending nine hours trying to work out a way of doing something which will earn you £50 in one hour, rather than just doing some boring job for £5 an hour for ten hours and not exercising your brain. Eric says we simply don't use our brains enough, and I'm sure he's right. I once read a psychology book in which — well, actually, a boyfriend of mine once had a psychology book *on his bedside table* which I didn't exactly *read*, more sort of looked at and got the vibes off — but anyway, this book said that we are all like sheep. Sheep. Actually, maybe it wasn't a psychology book at all, maybe it was a sort of mystic vibes book. I can't quite remember. But the point was that we are all like sheep. Because sheep spend their entire lives with this shepherd who pretends that he has their best interests at heart, only all the time he fully intends to send them to the market to be bought and slaughtered and then eaten with mint sauce. The sheep know this to be the set-up, but they make a point of not thinking about it, in order not to go stark staring mad. Well, you would, wouldn't you? And we are exactly like those sheep, according to this book. Because we go through our lives all carefree and contented, when all the time we know we are going to die, and if we had any sense we would do some really serious thinking about figuring out ways in which we might maybe be able to fix things so that we *wouldn't* die. Marvellous stuff. I got KY all over the front cover, and the boyfriend in question never forgave me, but that's another story. (But remind me to tell you about him later: he was Asian and had lovely dark skin, beautiful clothes, a great bum and a boyfriend of his own who he was cheating on. I must say I rather liked him. Whenever he came back to my place he would ring up his boyfriend to tell him that he was cheating on him and that the boyfriend wasn't to worry when he didn't get back home that night. I can't be sure, of course, but I have always imagined the boyfriend would say something like, "Oh, OK, Yogesh," (because that was his name, Yogesh) "have a nice time cheating on me, don't forget to use a condom and I'll see you tomorrow." So there's me falling in love with this beautiful Asian boy with lovely skin, and there's him on the phone to his husband making all the necessary arrangements before he is free to get into my bed. Well, it was fun at first. Eric says life's like that. Either you love them and they don't love you, or they love you and you don't love them. And we just have to wait until it all falls into place, like the three lemons coming up on the fruit machine, he says. *Three* lemons? say I. What's the third? What do you mean, what's the third? says he. I mean (say I) if *one* lemon is *you* loving *them*, and the *second* lemon is *them* loving *you, what is the third lemon?* Ah, says Eric, the *third lemon*. The third lemon is — but I'll have to tell you what Eric says the third lemon is later, because I'm still in brackets and it's giving me anxiety.)

The church my aunt took me to was lively, that cannot be denied. People would speak in tongues, and heal people, and that sort of thing. Once a black lady with cancer of the bowels was healed. She went into a little side-chapel or vestry or something and came out all healed, holding this squashy, jelly-like black thing in a paper towel. It didn't smell very nice. I think the idea was that *that was the cancer*, but it seems to me, looking back on it, now that I have had my faith conclusively rammed out of me by Eric's lovely boyfriend Corey (among others), that it was more likely to be a rotten pig's liver or something. But let that be. The point is that, every Sunday, and upon a number of weekdays besides, it was my God-given and joy-inducing task to go from door to door in the Hammersmith and Shepherds Bush neck of the woods spreading the good news about Father God and Christ Jesus. We didn't just call him God, we called him "Father God". And for reasons too perverse ever to be fathomed, we also always made a point of not calling Jesus Christ "Jesus Christ" but "Christ Jesus". I once had a theory that the senior members of the church had decided that, since the smash-hit success of the marvellous rock-opera *Jesus Christ Superstar*, the name "Jesus Christ" had been deprived of some of its former mystery. I know my father felt this to be the case. But whether that was why we all called him Christ Jesus or not I have never been able to ascertain with any tolerable degree of certainty. Actually, it doesn't really matter when the chips are down, does it?

TWO

"The third lemon," says Eric, deliberately spooning six spoonfuls of sugar into his tea, "is when neither of you is on the run from the Immigration Police."

Here is how Eric drinks his tea: first he pours in the tea and the milk, then he adds two teaspoonfuls of sugar. Then he takes a sip. He savours the tea thoughtfully, swallows, pauses for a moment with a kind of faraway look in his eyes, and then adds another spoonful. Another sip. Swallow; pause; a moment's indecision. The fourth spoonful. Same routine. Now the tea seems to be to some extent satisfactory. Minutes will pass. A couple more sips. Then finally spoonful five and spoonful six will hit the tea in fairly quick succession. I think the feeling at this point is: *OK, I admit it, I wanted six spoonfuls all along and the time has finally come to throw pretence to the winds and just whop in the full quota.* He does this not just sometimes but *every time*. Once I read a book on human behaviour — in fact I have read loads — and my studies have taught me that this is a classic example. Of human behaviour, I mean.

I also read a book about sugar.

"What *on earth* are you talking about?" I enquire, hastily closing the lid of the tupperware pot of condemned hazelnuts.

(Note: I have completely forgotten our conversation about life being like a fruit machine.)

"The third lemon is when neither of you is on the run from the —"

"I *heard* you," I reply, a little tartly. "I'm not *deaf*. It's just that I didn't understand a *single word*."

Eric looks up from his tea. He looks a little doleful (NB: remind me to tell you about Eric's dolefulness later; *crucial character information*). "*You know*," he replies; "the first lemon is when you love the guy; the second lemon is when the guy loves you, and the third lemon is when neither of you is on the run from the Immigration Police."

Scales fall from my eyes. It now seems to me that I have snapped at Eric without justification. Seasoned in the art of repartee, I change tack: "Talking of lemons," I begin in a no-nonsense tone, "I bought two apples yesterday. I put them on my shelf in the vegetable rack. I ate one. Where is the other?"

"I didn't eat it," says he. "Actually I didn't know we were meant to have our own shelves in the vegetable rack."

I sigh in exasperation. "Then no wonder my apple has disappeared," I tell him.

"But I don't even like apples!" he objects.

"That's not the point," I snap. "The point is, if people don't know that we have all got our own shelf on the vegetable rack, how can any of us hope to keep track of the food we've bought?"

Actually the problem is more complex. As no one knows for sure who is living in the house, it is in fact quite, quite impossible to work out any coherent system of personalized shelves in the vegetable rack, *let alone the fridge*. The pot of hazelnuts is not the only noisome by-product of this curious impasse. There is a red pepper in the "crisper" section of the fridge which has evidently not been properly irradiated and is showing signs of decay after only ten weeks. Luckily for us all, Eric works in the local community health council on a job-share scheme (he does two-and-a-half days) and his experience there has given him valuable abilities in the art of committee-chairing. We are about to have a House Meeting at which everything will be sorted out. The hazelnuts, the pepper, the whole problem of the mice, plus other problems such as the fact that the house is absolutely *filthy* and also no one logs their telephone calls. Everyone in the house has promised to be present. So far there's only me and Eric, but I talked to Tookie earlier on and she promised promised promised.

In the event there are three of us: Me, Eric, and our Swedish flatmate Bjorn. Eric opens the Minutes Book.

"Present at the meeting?" he asks, pencil poised.

"Me, you and Bjorn," I reply in my sort of official voice. I think I am the secretary or something.

Eric writes in the book: *Eric, Lenny, Bjorn*. (That's my name, Lenny). Then he looks up. "Apologies for absence?"

"None received," I reply.

None received, writes he.

"Now," says Eric, "we will start by reading the minutes of the last meeting."

"Very well," I reply.

"Can I just say that this pot of hazelnuts is extremely *unhigurnic*," whines Bjorn.

I sigh in exasperation, and inwardly flag at the prospect of explaining to Bjorn what a committee meeting is. His English is not watertight.

"We'll get to that in a minute," says Eric.

"That's what everyone always says!" objects the Swede. "Do you know what people would say about this house if it was in Sweden?"

"But it's not, is it?" I snap. "And anyway, if it was in Sweden you wouldn't have the Royal Oak just three minutes down the road, would you, or any of the other 101 other great places that make London the world's greatest city for same-sexers? Now just shut up and wait your turn!" After this speech of mine Bjorn goes very quiet, and I feel a bit guilty, because he's not really capable of sticking up for himself, and I have obviously *ridden him a bit hard*, as they say. Poor Bjorn spends most of his time closeted away in his room working on his CV. How he manages to spend so much time (approx four hours a day for the past two months) on what is after all only one side of A4 is an unending source of mystery to me. When I put this baffling question to Eric, he said somewhat darkly, "Maybe his CV needs a lot of work." Bjorn wants to be a highly-paid advertising executive. I am unable to comment on the question of whether his qualifications are equal to this ambition, because, of course, they are all Swedish. However, I fear the worst, as I feel that if his exam results were really all that they should be he would just need to whop 'em down and have done with it.

"The minutes of the last meeting are as follows," says Eric. "*Members present: Eric, Lenny, Tookie. Apologies for absence: None received. Agree the minutes for the last meeting: The minutes were agreed. Matters arising: There were none. Matters discussed: The matter of the free room...*"

I am amazed. "What free room?" I interrupt.

"You know," says Eric, "the one on the half-landing between the first and second floors. Peter's old room."

"Has Peter moved out?" I am triply amazed.

"Peter went back to Ireland in August," Eric explains patiently. (Note: it is now December.)

"Oh," I reply. "Well, he never said goodbye to me."

"He didn't say goodbye to anyone. He didn't leave us anything for the phone either."

"But isn't that Canadian boy in the room on the half-landing between the first and second floors?" I insist. As you will probably have gathered by now, it is rather a big house.

"I must say I thought so," says Eric; "but not according to these minutes. Listen..." And he reads. "*It was agreed that an advertisement would be put up in the First Out cafe. Also, other forms of networking within the Community would be employed. Applicants for the room would be required to submit CVs. A shortlisting panel would be set up. The CVs would be anonymized prior to circulation among the shortlisting panel. Interviews would follow after a period of three weeks had elapsed following the placing of the advertisement. It was agreed that Equal Opportunities interviewing techniques would be used: that is to say, straight applicants wouldn't have a snowballs's chance in hell of getting a room in our marvellous house–*"

"Just a minute," I interrupt. "Who put that bit in?"

"Peter," says Eric. "But you have to remember that Peter had a lot of anger in him. He still hasn't progressed beyond Identity Pride."

I am intrigued.

"Fascinating," I reply. "I had never thought of it like that before. And what comes after Identity Pride?"

Eric sighs dolefully. "Identity Integration, as you very well know," he tells me. "There are six stages in the progress of the same-sexer towards enlightenment. Denial, Tolerance, Acceptance, Pride and Integration. Now can we get on with the meeting, please?"

Now, Eric is an absolutely fascinating character. A prime example of human psychology if ever I saw one. He is a marvellous man, tall and fit and clever and serene. And what's more he has the most beautiful boyfriend a man could hope for: Corey, after whom we all lust nightly, breaker of a zillion hearts, Eros personified. And yet for all this he is doleful. Not downright wrist-slashing, but just *a little bit doleful all the time*, as if he carries on his shoulders a heavy burden which he wants to set down but for some reason cannot. I often see my role as being Eric's cheerer-up, which is absurd really, because Eric has so much more going for him than me. If I had Eric's body and Eric's boyfriend I wouldn't be complaining, I can tell you. I once asked him if he had ever had to work out much to get his body the way it is (big and bear-like with not an ounce of fat), and he said No, not much, it just sort of grew when he was seventeen. Just grew! Don't ask me about the hours I have spent pitting my wits against fiendish arrangements of weights and pulleys, only to end up looking exactly the same as I looked before I started, which is to say, like a little spring lamb. (But more about me later.) You could almost imagine Eric modelling swimwear for Marks and Spencer, except I suppose that his nose is rather large and his chin is on the small side, which makes him look a tiny bit like a llama. (Note: maybe that's why he's doleful. Memo: go to library — psychology section — find out about effect of slight resemblance to llama on personality.)

"That was five," I point out.

"Five what?"

"Denial, Acceptance, Tolerance, Pride and Integration," I repeat. "That's five. You said there were six."

"What about the cleaning rota?" says Bjorn. "I can't live in a dirty house. This is not *higurnic*."

Now, at the risk of sounding a tiny tad vindictive, I must report that there is a reality gap between Bjorn's oft-voiced concern with hygiene and the nitty-gritty truth about his personal habits.

1) He never ever does any cleaning at all.

2) He leaves soggy teabags in the sink (yeugh!), all mixed in with the washing-up he hasn't done.

3) He refuses to stack the cutlery upright in our marvellous yellow plastic upright cutlery-drainer, accusing it of being *unhigurnic* on the grounds that all the water from the cutlery is going to drain downwards and collect in a pool at the bottom, which is then going to stand like a brackish pond and presumably breed mosquitoes and other foul monsters. I have actually shown him the holes in the bottom of our wonderful cutlery-drainer, but he is Adam Ant. So he leaves wet cutlery lying around on the draining-board, and heaven knows what micro-ecologies flourish in the little pools of water that remain in the up-turned spoons.

4) Most heinously of all, he comes straight in from the street and curls up on the sofa *with his shoes still on*, grinding the contents of the London pavements into what was once a perfectly respectable piece of furniture.

Well, that is his hygiene record, and I personally don't think he scores ten out of ten. But what *really gets me* is the way he invites his Swedish friends round to dinner and then *apologizes to them* about how horrid the house is. It does seem to me that

a) If you think it's so horrid, why live here? and

b) If it's really so intolerable, why not pick up the hoover once every six months?

But let that be.

The meeting is eventually over, and the minutes read as follows:

Present at the meeting: Eric, Lenny, Bjorn.

Apologies for absence: None received.

Agree the minutes for the last meeting: The minutes were agreed.

Matters arising: There were none.

Matters discussed: The matter of the pot of hazelnuts was discussed. It was agreed that no solution could be found until such time as every member of the household was present together at one time. The matter of the mice was discussed. It was agreed that presence of mice in the house was *unhigurnic* and not to be tolerated. The matter of the house being absolutely filthy was discussed. Members agreed that a new cleaning rota should be drawn up at the next meeting. It was also agreed that instead of just sticking a rota up on the wall like last time, members of the household should perhaps actually do the jobs specified. It was agreed that a cleaning rota is a cleaning rota, not a pretty picture. It was agreed that if we wanted pretty pictures we would go to Athena.

THREE

The four months I spent staying with my aunt in Chiswick were not materially different from the years I had spent at home, only now I was within sight of the Promised Land. I was expected to be home each evening by ten, which rather put a damper on any midnight *Wanderlust* to which as a growing boy I was bound to be prone, but London by day was sufficient to awaken my curiosity. It did not escape my notice that alternatives seemed to exist to procreation and holy home-making, and that, indeed, many of them were "at loose" (as my father no doubt would have put it) in the Hammersmith streets. I was like a starving man looking at a hot dinner through a thick pane of glass. I see now that my father's principle of keeping his tender offspring out of the metropolis at all costs was not without its own fiendish logic. I think he felt there was a very real danger that if we went to London we might *become interested in something* — it didn't matter what. Any sort of interest would be enough to burst the bubble of permanent tedium in which our entire lives had been led. I doubt whether he would have predicted the precise nature of *my* specialist interest, but then, that's what life's like in the real world. Full of surprises.

During my evenings alone in my room, I studied the Holy

Scriptures with increased vigour, vaguely aware of being under attack from the Evil One and feeling that, as I was probably going to give in to him within the very foreseeable future, I might as well give my big old dog-eared Bible one last chance to prove that it wasn't the random compilation of superstitious rantings that I was beginning to suspect it was.

My job (as a clerk in a recruitment consultancy) was a disappointment; after a honeymoon period of a few weeks, the glamour faded and I was left bored out of my skull, filing CVs and slaving over a juddering photocopier. The tedium of my work was so extreme as to make my evangelical duties appear positively fun-packed.

I worked in an office with two wonderful women called Alice and Paula. They were good at their job and I admired them terrifically. They power-dressed. In a way it was a privilege to do their photocopying, but always at the back of my mind was the nagging awareness that I was destined for higher things — that my soul needed to breathe an air more rarified than that which circulated in the corridors of the Open Door Recruitment Agency. I think Alice and Paula sensed this too. Once when we were relaxing at lunchtime over baguettes and cottage cheese, Alice gave a sad little sigh and said to me, "Oh Lenny, I can tell you're not happy here. We're just not glamorous enough for you, are we?"

I didn't know what to say. I loved them both dearly, but in a way she was right. I had to move on. But where? Little did I know that in a few months time I would be living in a house which was in many ways the intellectual centre of London. (An interesting note here: one of the great advantages of living at the very centre of what is really *happening* and *going on*, as we do, is that there's a sense in which

1) every day's a holiday, and

2) you never know who's going to walk in through the door next).

Soon after the House Meeting has been adjourned, Tookie comes in (Apologies for absence: None received), and introduces us all to a friend she has brought with her, a young actress called Barbara Honigsbaum who is just about to become extremely famous! Perhaps I should explain. Tookie runs this exciting, go-ahead young agency called *Stars of the Future*, and she's very hyped up about the whole thing at the moment because it really looks like she's finally going to be able to get herself an office and not have to work from home any more, which frankly hasn't really been all that satisfactory in many ways, I mean you can imagine why, what with us all sharing one phone and Tookie naturally having important calls just about to come through from Hollywood all the time and therefore (quite understandably) liable to snap at anyone who might stay on the phone for longer than about a minute at a time. We are all delighted to meet Barbara Honigsbaum, who looks a bit like a giraffe but is undoubtedly very beautiful, and wonder whether we should celebrate in some way the double good news of

a) the probable office and

b) Barbara, who has *star* written all over her, joining the team.

Tookie's other client (is that the word?) is Eric, of course, an absolutely riveting actor who I am outraged to say hasn't delighted a live audience for well over eighteen months. The polite term for this is *at rest*. Eric is an actor *at rest*. He's not *out of work*, merely *at rest*. I remember when I first moved into the house, Eric was in a totally stunning thing at the King's Head about a man who was in love with this other man (both cowboys!) who didn't love him, but he sort of *forced* him to love him, and the way he did this was the most appalling way you could possibly imagine, but utterly true and value-challenging. What he did was, he sort of persuaded the man who didn't love him to nail him to the doors of his barn, and then go to the graveyard and dig up the body of a third man, who had previously been *both* of their boyfriends while he was alive, and whom the second man (the one who didn't love the first man) had shot after the third man had confessed to him that he was only his (the second man's) boyfriend because the fiendish *first* man had set him up to it *so that he could get at the second man*, who he was now really cross with for not loving him — to dig up the dead body of the third man and bring him round to the first man's house and *show him* the first man nailed to the barn doors, thus in some perverse way expiating the guilt which the first man felt for having indirectly caused the third man's death. After doing all this the second man fell in love with the first man (well, you would, wouldn't you?), except by this time it didn't really count because he'd gone mad (the second man, that is.) At least, that's how I "read" it. But the crucifixion scene was incredible — the actor took all his clothes off and you could see his dick and everything. I suppose one shouldn't really say it (probably shouldn't even *think* it) but in a horrid and of course pretty value-challenging way it was actually rather a turn-on, what with the fake blood and the dick and everything. For weeks afterwards I had dreams about being crucified by handsome men (don't tell my Dad!!) in cowboy outfits. Luckily, it wasn't Eric who had to take his clothes off. Eric played the dead body.

So there we all are wondering which particular pleasure-train to ride.

I open the bidding. "Well, it's either a quick heads-round-the-door visit to the Royal Oak, or we *could* go the whole hog and take in the mud-wrestling at the City Apprentice. I mean, are we celebrating or are we celebrating?"

"I wouldn't mind the mud-wrestling," says Eric, "but I'm not going unless we all go, because it's a taxi-ride back, and let's face it, there's not a lot of money about these days."

Barbara Honigsbaum says something very polite which makes it abundantly clear that she has not the faintest intention of going anywhere near the mud-wrestling. I am a little disappointed by this, as I actually find the mud-wrestling quite artistic in a way, but say nothing, having previously done a fair amount of reading on the subject of non-confrontational group-decision-making. Our options are gradually narrowing down. It is now a choice between the Royal Oak (Saturday night, very crowded, smoky) or staying in and lighting some candles and turning off the lights. Suddenly we all realize that we have a quarter of a bottle of rum and a can of Seven-Up, and at this point the scales tip right down in favour of the candle-lit evening-in option.

After a while we are all very mellow and have taken off our shoes and are luxuriating in a special tape compilation I have made of transmissions from the planet Fargon as picked up by the quill-shaped receiver of the divine Wolfgang Amadeus. Tookie tells us all about the office she's probably going to get (above a feminist bookshop) and what an incredible boost to business it's going to represent. Tookie's hair is particularly fine this evening, all sort of tied up with spikes through it like she's from some weird tribe from Mars with completely different values from ours. OK, so we smoke some dope. We happen to think it's less toxic than alcohol. If you don't agree, just get off our backs, OK? Later Eric impulsively makes some spaghetti. Unfortunately the evening is sort of ruined by Barbara stepping on a slug in her bare feet. That's another thing that's wrong with the house. We do occasionally get giant slugs that come out at night, and they're not very easy to see by candle-light. Shit — *I'm still in brackets!!)*

"Oh, don't be silly, Alice, of course you're glamorous — terribly," I replied, in such a way as to imply that I was politely skirting round a less palatable truth. (Note: we are now back in the Open Door Recruitment Agency. Sorry. Sorry.) You see, I knew I was going to have to abandon them sooner or later, and I wanted to prepare them for the shock.

"You're too good for photocopying and making tea and things," said Paula. "You need something more creative."

Creative! It was the first time I had been called creative in my entire life. I thrilled with pleasure.

"I don't know," I said. "Perhaps you're right. I *have* considered becoming a fireman, but I think perhaps I'm a bit small."

Don't ask me how tall I am. Just don't ask. OK, then, I'm 5'6". 5'6"! And don't ask me how much I weigh either. Actually, you might as well know. Ninety-eight pounds. Added to which, since the age of twelve I have looked as if I am twelve years old. The years pass but my appearance does not alter. Many people naively imagine that I am blessed in this, but to me it is a curse. In fact I firmly believe that this is the one factor that has prevented me from rising to executive positions in any of the careers in which I have dabbled. I have tried growing a beard, but that just makes me look like a twelve-year-old with a glued-on beard. Children laugh at me in the streets. Each night I pray for grey hairs and wrinkles (I believe that in this I am unique in the gay community).

The other thing that has prevented me from being called upon to take on the sort of responsibilities for which I am in every other way qualified is, I believe, my voice. Let's face it, my voice is just the worst. I have heard my voice recorded on tape a few times (I try to avoid this dubious pleasure whenever possible) and I have been struck on every occasion by its uncanny resemblance to the sounds made by a small furry animal crying for its mother. I have tried lowering it and speaking in grave, funereal tones, but to no avail. I still sound like a small furry animal crying for its mother. But let that rest. My life is full of excitement and stimulation, and I believe that it is very wrong to complain about what Nature in her infinite vibe-filled wisdom has seen fit to bestow upon us.

One of Satan's first tentative little strategies to lure me away from the True Path was to tempt my young and trusting heart into an interest in health foods. Just a few hundred yards down King Street from the Open Door Recruitment Agency was a shop selling every conceivable vegetarian delicacy you could possibly imagine, and I was to spend many an ecstatic lunch-hour wandering distractedly from shelf to musty shelf, filling brown paper bags with carob-coated raisins and nutritional yeast-flakes and dreaming of the orient East. I even tried to introduce brown rice into my aunt's scheme of things, but she, ever alert to the wiles of the Lord of the Flies, wisely dismissed such a radical challenge to the traditions of holy home-making as propaganda for the Antichrist. Given my current interest in Zen Buddhism, which can be traced directly back to a leaflet I picked up in the Hammersmith Wholefood Emporium, I think we must concede that she had a point.

Then one day I noticed a big hand-written sign in the window saying that they were looking for staff, and I hurried inside to make enquiries. I was given an application form and asked to fill it in. It went like this:

ANSWER ALL THE QUESTIONS. USE INK NOT PENCIL. USE BLOCK CAPITALS. ANSWER QUESTIONS (8) TO (10) AND QUESTIONS (18) TO (20) ON SEPARATE SHEETS. WRITE YOUR NAME AND THE DATE ON ANY SEPARATE SHEETS YOU ATTACH. ATTACH SEPARATE SHEETS BY PAPER-CLIP NOT STAPLE.

1) Are you married or single? (circle where applicable)
2) Are you male or female? (circle where applicable)
3) Are you gay or straight? (circle where applicable)
4) Do you have dependants? (if yes, give number)
5) What is your date of birth?
6) What is your age?
7) What are your qualifications?
8) Why do you think your qualifications are of relevance to the Hammersmith Wholefood Emporium? (separate sheet)
9) Give full details of your previous work experience, together with exhaustive details of any travel you may have undertaken (NB: conventional beach/disco holidays do not count) — (separate sheet)
10) Give an exhaustive list of any other special skills or personality traits you have or may *think you have*, which will be (or may, in your view, be) invaluable to the Hammersmith Wholefood Emporium. (separate sheet)
11) List your leisure interests. (Remember that watching TV is an occupation, not an interest)
12) State your philosophical and/or religious standpoint (separate sheet if necessary)
13) List any groups, political, social, or otherwise, of which you are now a member. Do not include health clubs in this list.
14) What hours of work are you looking for and why? (Remember that working at the Hammersmith Wholefood Emporium can be extremely strenuous mentally, physically and spiritually. We get many applications from people who are attracted to the "laid-back" atmosphere of the store. Nothing, in reality, could be further from the truth. We must stress that working at the Emporium is *not a soft option*. If we manage to make it look easy then that's just because we are working just that little bit harder.)
15) How long are you wanting to work with us — what are your future plans?
16) Are you willing to work early morning and late night shifts?
17) Are you willing to work on Saturdays?
18) In your own carefully-chosen words, state *what you perceive natural foods to mean*. (separate sheet)

19) Detail the food topics which you have knowledge of and *how the knowledge was acquired.* (separate sheet).

20) *Why* are you interested in working at the Hammersmith Wholefood Emporium? Think very carefully. (separate sheet)

21) Give the full names, addresses and phone numbers of at least four referees. State the capacity in which they are known to you. (Non-vegetarians will not be accepted as referees.)

I took the questionnaire home and hid it furtively in my room, along with my copy of *Myra Breckinridge* and an illustrated biography of Burt Lancaster. Soon now, soon now.

FOUR

It's funny how you can really hit it off with someone and feel that you're definitely going to be chums, and yet still find it impossible to resist deriving just a tiny amount of pleasure from the misfortunes which befall them. Barbara Honigsbaum, for example, beautiful and soon to be famous (but unfortunately just a little bit too delicately brought up for the mud-wrestling). Perhaps it is because I am stoned, but I can't help having a good old laugh (which I tactfully suppress and hide behind my sleeve) when she steps on the slug. ("What's this?" she says, picking the slug up and inspecting it uncertainly in the dim candlelight. There is quite a lot of food lying about on the floor — plates of cheese and bowls of grapes and things. Barbara thinks the slug is food. Everyone peers at the slug. We are all pretty stoned by this time and the old brain cells are dying off by the millions per second. "Feels sort of squishy . . . like a Turkish Delight or something. . ." She sniffs the slug. "Don't eat it if it's been on the floor, Barbara," says Tookie. "Here, have a smidgeon of Brie." Barbara deposits the slug onto a plate on the table and thinks no more of it. The conversation drifts back, slowly but inevitably, to the perennially fascinating subject of her forthcoming fame. There's this fab new director who's only twelve or something and he's just made a movie for only £1 and it's just grossed $500m in the States or something and Barbara has been "slated" to star in his new megabucks-smasheroo opposite an android made up of the top half of Tom Cruise and the bottom half of Mel Gibson, etc., etc., etc. The plate containing the slug is now directly under the candle and therefore brightly illuminated. After an interlude of who can tell how long (time has little meaning when you are scaling the steep cliff-faces of alternative enlightenment), someone comments upon how "far out" it is that the Turkish Delight is moving slowly across the plate leaving a trail of slime.)

"But would Barbara have had a horrid experience if she had never found out that it had been a slug all along, but had gone to her grave under the delusion that it had been a Turkish Delight? . . ."

Eric and I are sitting in the First Out enjoying banana-and-poppyseed slices and looking out for handsome Brazilian boys. (Note: later on: explore further philosophical implications of whole slug *debacle*; e.g., consider question: how many slugs has one *already eaten*, under similar circumstances, and remained none the wiser?) At least, *I* am looking out for Brazilian boys. Eric doesn't need a boyfriend — he has the lovely Corey, Eros personified, after whom we all lust nightly. But he is a generous soul, and he is helping me "look for a husband", as we only semi-ironically put it. (I shall discuss the complex matter of whether or not Eric is looking for opportunities to cheat on his lovely boyfriend in a later chapter.)

"How about him?" he murmurs discreetly. I look across the room. At a table near ours three alert-looking Brazilians are settling themselves down with plates of rather high-priced salad and maps of London. My mouth waters. I realize that I would probably kill for just one night with any of them. *What are my hormones up to?* I am obviously hallucinating. They are probably quite boring-looking in reality.

"Fuck!" I murmur hoarsely, threatened by overstimulation. "Which one?"

We discuss Brazilians. I distractedly wolf down my banana-and-poppyseed slice. Overstimulation strikes. I go to the washrooms and splash cold water on my face and neck (not enough privacy to douse the part that needs it most). I see my own absurd reflection in the mirror and curse impotently. I know full well that if I were one of the Brazilian boys I wouldn't want a little spring lamb, I would want some rough-and-ready tanned sporty type in a cowboy outfit. I decide to go back out into the cafe, go straight to our table without looking at the Brazilians and suggest to Eric that we go home. Beyond that I cannot plan. My pulse is racing.

When I get back to our table Corey is there. He is bubbling about his forthcoming trip to Amsterdam.

"The saunas are marvellous," he chirps. "There's group sex in the steam-rooms and little cubicles if you want to be private. And of course these places are choc-a-bloc with beautiful men. What more could one want?"

Eric and I are both terribly impressed by how attractive Corey is looking. He is wearing faded 501s, bum-hugging (don't look! don't look!) and tastefully ripped above one of the knees to let a thrilling gash of milky flesh peep out, soft and pure, unlike my thoughts. His jacket makes you think of the Air Force and dog-fights and things, and his hair is short short SHORT, with a little miniature quiff perched somewhat ironically on his forehead, like a small rodent. As always, his eyes are bright as he banters of this and that (mostly that) in his irrepressible way.

Now, at first I was rather naive about S-E-X and I believed that one hundred per cent of the people in the world wanted one thing and one thing only, namely to fall in love with a handsome man or willowy girlie and have sex with that one person and no one else for the rest of their lives. Don't laugh! — how was I to know? No one talked about sex in my family. I was left to cobble together my own map of this particular twilight zone from:

a) the few references to the topic grudgingly offered by the Holy Scriptures (for some reason my copy of the Good Book always had a tendency to fall open at the bit about David and Jonathan — sometimes *at prayer meetings*, blush blush!)

b) gossip

c) Burt Lancaster movies

d) *Pride and Prejudice*, which was my O-level English text. Well, you can imagine what a recipe for disaster this all was. My naiveté knew no bounds.

I know better now, of course. I have read (or at least, dipped into) many fascinating and well-researched books on the subject, and I have sat at the feet of my flatmate and mentor the wise and witty Eric, who has been so good as to share with me the many insights which he has gleaned over his many years as a practising (regarding which vexed word, more later) same-sexer — pearls which, swine-like, I have snaffled greedily up.

The point of this diversion is that *Eric is not going to Amsterdam with Corey*. Simply not going! And you know why not? Because Eric and Corey have an *open relationship*. Corey is going to go to Amsterdam *on his own*, and go to the saunas, and have group sex in the steam-rooms and then some private sex in a cubicle (he'll be terribly good and use a condom at all times of course), and all this with the most marvellously handsome men you could possibly imagine. And why not? Corey just happens to like men, that's all. All sorts of men — dark hair, light hair, big dick, little dick (within reason) — he just loves 'em all. Corey is young and quite irresistible and he just happens to feel that life is too short for a boy *not* to make full use of the opportunities with which Nature — in her infinite, vibe-filled om-ness — has seen fit to profusely strew his path (and of which I myself was one, though probably the least exciting). I understand now that the romantic dreams of a virgin teenage swot are of no more relevance to the real world than the moons and stars on a sorcerer's hat; that the very concept of monogamy is "just another brick in the Wall" (to quote a transmission from the planet Fargon as received via the guitar-shaped receivers of the ineffable Pink Floyd); and that our only hope for full development as human beings and temples of the Holy Vibe of the Age of Aquarius is to obey the dictates of our instincts as readily as if we were the Hitler Youth and they were the Führer.

There will of course be those for whom the dawning of the New Age will be not without its traumas — who will have to be dragged kicking and screaming (as it were) into the party. Me, for example. And Eric too, come to think of it, though to a lesser extent. Both Eric and I have secretly admitted to each other, in moments of great candour and high brain-cell death-rate, that we are in many ways less evolved than Corey. Or, to use a marvellous old word, more *hung-up*. About sex, I mean. We both share this thing about being a bit, well, shy I suppose. It's not that we don't actually want to sleep with half of the male population of Brazil — we do — it's just that we can never seem to get it together. Call us old-fashioned. It's true. We belong to the old breed and — thank goodness for the planet! — the old breed is dying out.

"So what have you two been up to?" pipes Corey in his inimitable breezy way. "Trying to find Lenny a husband, I'll be darned!"

"You read our minds," we laugh.

"Any luck?" says he, looking round the room with a frankness that makes my ears burn. "Holy shit! Have you seen what I see?" Corey has spotted the Brazilians. "Now that's what I call sex!"

"We had . . . um . . . noticed them," I mutter, playing with my cold teabag and wondering if I will *ever* be as evolved as Corey.

Eric smiles benignly. "What is going on in that lecherous little mind of yours, Corey?" he demands in mock seriousness. I am always most impressed by the amazing tact with which Eric handles these situations. In terms of evolution, I suppose he must be about halfway between me and his boyfriend. Corey flashes him a little loving smile that makes me jealous of their happiness. "Either of you guys want them?" he politely enquires. I realize with some shock (but also with admiration) that he intends to have *all three*.

"Um . . . no . . . no," I mutter. "I'm, er, not in the mood."

"See if I care," says Eric, with a mock-pout.

Corey springs up, walks over to the table where the Brazilians are and, apparently without so much as an opening gambit, sits down. After a few moments they are all having a jolly good laugh about something, and a minute later (or so it seems — time is hard to judge when you can't believe your eyes) they all get up together and leave. Being not remotely evolved enough to be able to handle the delicate niceties of life in an open relationship, I pretend not to have noticed (difficult). (Note: the subject of Eric and Corey's open relationship is absolutely fascinating and I promise promise promise to return to it later.)

We finish our food and are soon obliged by the excruciating discomfort of the seats to leave — a clever bit of cafe-management on First Out's part, this, as they understandably don't want customers hanging around for three-and-a-half hours putting in some serious time waiting for "Mr Right" to walk through the door (another "brick in the wall" concept foolishly adopted from the heterosexual patriarchy, of course), while making a single banana-and-poppyseed slice last.

On the way home we pass a beautiful man in the street with ginger hair and white trousers. I look back and he's looking back at us! My pulse races. A second glance, however, is enough to ascertain that it is Eric he fancies, and, as Eric feels, maybe old-fashionedly, that one boyfriend is enough, we walk on. "The next one will be for you," says Eric, ever considerate of my feelings. There isn't a next one.

We get home. I have to be at the restaurant by five, and I plan on curling up on the sofa for a couple of hours with a book on the effects on the personality of looking like a llama, if I can find one, and a soothing cup of camomile tea. Essential to unwind before an evening of stress at the beck and call of a restaurant-full of hungry and sometimes also lecherous same-sexers. When we get back, Bjorn is curled up on the sofa with his shoes on, grinding (one fears) fresh dog shit into our once-rather-nice sofa. I bite back a whinnying scream of frustration and rage (having once read, sorry, *dipped into*, a book about *living with people*) and retire to my room. On the stairs is a letter from my father, which provokes a marvellously stimulating discussion between me and Eric on the subject of the spelling of the word 'practising'. In his letter, my father speaks of his shock and concern at having gleaned (whether on the grapevine or via a hot-line direct to Him Who Is To Be Obeyed one dare not speculate) that I am living in a household of *practising homosexualists*. My father, we note, has plumped for *practising* with an 's'. Eric insists that the word should have two 'c's. At first I am inclined to side with my father (rare).

"The noun is *practice*; the verb is *practise*," I pronounce in a tone intended to be firm but not patronizing.

"Not necessarily," says he. "My years of experience in the Community Health Council have taught me otherwise. Many doctors insist on keeping the 's' out of the verb as well, to emphasize the fact that when they 'practise', they are not, for example, keeping their arpeggios up to scratch on the piano.

They are running a *practice*. It's a completely different verb, and they quite deliberately spell it with two 'c's."

My mind reels at the subtlety of his argument. For a moment I have to concentrate on my poster of Burt Lancaster in *The Killers* (Robert Siodmak, 1946) just to stop my brain from overloading. "Which sense do you think my father meant?" I ask. "The doctor's surgery sense or the musical instrument sense?"

We decide that my father must have had a vision of some hellish doctor's surgery with fiends dressed as nurses holding struggling under-age victims down while Beelzebub himself, thinly disguised behind a stethoscope and an expression of mock-concern, cracks a popper before administering medicine of a type too abominable to be set forth in words. . .

As we laugh, I marvel (vaguely, at the back of my mind) at how sophisticated I have become since leaving home.

FIVE

So there I was, trudging around Shepherds Bush in my Sunday best with my "brother" Barney (church-brother, that is, not real brother), knocking on the doors of innocent citizens who had done nothing to deserve being hassled by spiritual fascists, and waving my executive-style plasticated identity card in their faces whenever they were unwise enough to open their doors, with the words, "Hello we're from the local church and were just wondering whether you were interested in Father God or Christ Jesus at all and whether you might like to invite them into your life at all and if not whether you might like to talk about it at all and if not *why not* and if not not NOT then is there anyone else in the house who you think *might* be interested in Father God or Christ Jesus . . . at all?" I think most of the honest citizens of Shepherds Bush were far too terrified by my intrusion (little twelve-year-old spring lamb with a false beard glued on and a mad, staring look in the eyes) to show any hostility.

Barney and I would take it in turns to ring the doorbell. I think perhaps, looking back on it, that he was better at it than me. More credible. He was a mild soul, a bit spotty but quite pleasant in a boring sort of way. He looked like a bloodhound. I may as well confess here and now that the converts we made were few and far between. A lot of people were quite prepared to talk to us, but it was mainly to tell us why they *wouldn't* be coming to church and inviting either Father God or Christ Jesus into their lives. The general feeling seemed to be one of slightly carping bitterness about the way they had been treated by both of these two once popular idols (we never mentioned the hugely embarrassing Holy Spirit — supposedly just as fab and glamorous as the rest of the trinity but in actual fact, as everyone deep down knew, coming in a very poor third); people talked to us as if we were representatives of, for instance, British Telecom, and they wanted us to carry word back to our boss that they were pretty dissatisfied with the service they'd been getting. I would try to explain to them that *each one of us* can have a hotline to Father God if he only asks — a wicked falsehood really, considering it was something that I had never believed myself, not even in the most rabid throes of my holy fervour. "Christ Jesus is just waiting to come into your life," I would bleat; "all you have to do is ask." This, I suppose, I did believe, up to a point: Christ Jesus was very much "in" my life, though to be absolutely strict about it my "asking him in" had been pretty much a formality. He had been there all along in my family household, sitting like a toad in our midst, solid and immovable. Never any question about whether one might like to ask him to *leave*.

After a hard Sunday morning on the streets, Barney and I would go back to my aunt's pad, where a fab lunch would be waiting (heterosexual patriarchy, all is forgiven!) and then retire to my room to indulge in thrillingly speculative theological discussion. We also shared our most intimate thoughts and feelings (bar a few) about how our relationships with Christ Jesus were progressing — our disgust with ourselves for having sinned (you've always sinned with Christ Jesus, even when you haven't), our plans for new and more efficient forms of self-discipline and our hopes for converts. Sometimes we went to movies together. We never hung round discos, and we never talked about girls. I suppose we were just too damn holy — or at least, that must have been Barney's excuse.

Where are you now, Barney? Sometimes my thoughts fly to you on cold winter nights by the gas-fire when I am warmed by dope truffles and hessian-wrapped Rioja and find myself overwhelmed by the feeling that all is forgiven. Mum — Dad — all you bastards who "taught" me (ha!) — Aunt Amber — all you scheming fascists at the church, impenetrably disguised as mild purveyors of tea and digestive biscuits — and you, Barney, maybe you most of all — forgiven, forgiven, forgiven! Where are you now? No doubt propping up the patriarchy with the sweat of your brow, no doubt exploited, no doubt procreating. Keep it up, me old mucker, keep it up! Between you and me, that old patriarchy of yours probably needs all the propping up it can get, so don't let me stand in your way with my wild subversive ideas and my alternative "lifestyle". Do you ever pause in the supermarket aisles, as you linger between *Whiskas* and *Kit-e-Kat* (your mousy wife no doubt great with her zillionth child) and wonder *Whatever happened to old Lenny*? Lenny who you had a few laughs with — admit it!

Ah, the gentle deceptions of marijuana! I am sure that if Barney and I met by chance on some rain-splashed Hammersmith street-corner we would have very little to say to each other now, very little in common. Maybe we never did. (We were, after all, "assigned" to each other). But we'd probably have *even less* in common now that he (at a wild guess) is working his way thrustingly up through the ranks of the tellers in Barclays Bank, while I am content, for the present, with my humble niche in the catering profession, secure in the knowledge that some day (and it is very much in the nature of my philosophy *not to rush these things*) my life will spontaneously blossom and bloom into something very different, full of strange new opportunities — foreign countries, dark-haired men, money, success, fame and glamour! Maybe it will be some earth-shattering insight gained while smoking marijuana. Maybe some key-to-the-door connection made while serving that last Tia Maria to a blissfully satisfied zillionaire at the restaurant — who knows? But between Barney and me lies a great gulf.

Eric says you must always try to forgive, and Lord! how true it is. "You simply have to," he says, "for the sake of your karma."

I must say when I first heard Eric talking about karma I didn't know *what* he was rabbiting on about; now, of course, I consider myself to be something of an expert on the subject. Eric lent me this book called *Blinded by the Light*, which, joking apart, *really is* a transcript of a transmission from outer space, which was picked up by a Danish husband-and-wife team while in a trance state. *Blinded by the Light* is, I suppose you could say, Eric's Bible, and frankly what's good enough for Eric is good enough for me. It contains detailed descriptions of heaven (including some amazing revelations about how the universe is not actually as big as Western Science would have us believe — Western Science has been fooled, you see, by the presence of these sort of *giant mirror-type things* hanging in space that make the universe look infinite, when actually it's not); also a lot of very good stuff about the need to be nice to people and not use the office photocopier without asking permission (and to *speak up* when shop assistants give you too much change rather than taking it home and then blowing it on beer 'n boys); and finally a whole section about what happens to us when we die, which I must say cut right through the bullshit as far as I was concerned. We are, of course, reincarnated — which is all right by me if it means that maybe next time I won't look like a spring lamb. And it also means, of course, that if we don't *quite* get our shit together in this life, we can sort of take things up from where we left off when we are born back into the world. Obviously we won't have the same bank account or anything, but if we have *evolved spiritually*, this *will* make a difference. We will be that little bit wiser, more together. So, contrary to what many a bourgeois pedagogue would have you believe, there *is* a certain amount of point to lounging about getting stoned at the expense of the supposedly more "serious" things in life, *as long as you get stoned in a philosophical way*, which Eric and I always do, and Tookie does when she has the energy — but she's usually so shattered after a hard day of waiting for phone-calls from Hollywood, poor dear, that all she can face is *recreational* drug-abuse, which of course is quite different. This whole matter of reincarnation goes a long way towards explaining such previously inexplicable phenomena as, for example, people's differing attitudes towards sex. Now, it is quite clear that Corey, for instance, must have been at least a Mayan High Priest in his previous life, whereas Eric was probably just a minor French aristocrat at the court of Louis XIV and I must have been something like a centipede.

One of the other waiters at Van Rijn's (where I work three or four shifts a week — sorry, couldn't face the full six) has read *Blinded by the Light* as well, and we have a lot of fun reliving favourite passages. He is absolutely convinced he was Marie Antoinette, but I think to be brutal there's an element of wishful thinking in that. Now, for reasons too potentially harrowing to be inquired into with any degree of persistence, all the waiters at Van Rijn's insist on being called by girls' names. (Gay Lib is obviously alive and well in Fulham, I don't think.) The fact that Van Rijn's is a restaurant for same-sexers has never seemed to me to be an adequate excuse for this frightening lunacy. There is a blond Irish waiter (long flowing hair, "subtle" make-up) called Patricia; a dark Irish waiter (quite reasonable-looking) called Kate; and a cute South African boy (tanned, quite sporty-looking) who I would rather fancy if only he didn't introduce himself to you as Anthea. When I first met the assistant chef and was told he was called Bibi, I naturally assumed that he too had been driven to distraction by same-sex orientation, but as frolicsome Fate would have it, this transpired to be untrue. Bibi is Moroccan, extremely beautiful and (razors poised over your wrists, guys) STRAIGHT. The "Bibi" business is to do with being Moroccan, apparently. What makes matters even less tolerable is he's also really nice and *likes* me — you know — *as a person*. I suffer the tortures of the damned. Each time I go to work, I wait for 6pm, mouth watering and knees a-tremble. Because at that precise hour Bibi *changes his T-shirt*. It is therefore absolutely vital (at least, it is to me), to be *in the bar, with the door to the kitchen open* at the moment when the clock strikes six. I have cleverly fixed things so that it is my job to clean the downstairs bit of the restaurant, which is a bummer in the sense that you have to do the loos, but it does mean that you get to do the bar, and so if you time things right you're laughing. What you do is, you finish cleaning the loos around 5.58, go into the kitchen to return the bleach and accidentally-on-purpose wedge the door open as you go out. Then you get the bar-cleaning stuff, walk round and stand with a cloth in your hand and look as if you are intently polishing some bit that's probably already clean anyway, but that's not the point; the point is *you're there*, view completely unobstructed, and it doesn't matter if Patrick (the owner) suddenly bursts in unexpectedly from some quarter — you're safe, because even though you are a million miles away, on some hot desert shore greedily chewing on the fantastic Bibi's nut-brown nipples while palm-trees sway and camels doze, you *look busy*.

Now I know it's important to be forgiving and I'll probably come back as a wood-louse for saying so, but Patrick, I must say, is a complete plop. I don't know, it's just something about the way he swishes about the restaurant barking orders at everyone in his phoney high-class accent, it gets up my nose. I had a fair idea that he fancied my ass when he gave me the job but I didn't think he'd be so sleazy as to pinch it while I was attempting to serve his customers. Actually, I deserve it. I confessed that I had no experience when I went for the interview, and flattered myself that he would employ me for my decorative value. Naiveté, thy name is Lenny. Was. When I first put on my waiter outfit and checked myself in the mirror I was thrilled. My hair was freshly bleached and my shoes were shiny-black and new. I had a white shirt on and a little black bow-tie. I loved myself. I drifted about the empty restaurant practising lines which I fondly imagined I would have the time and the bollocks to use — "May I recommend the *plat du jour*? Chef is particularly proud of it!" — "Something to drink while you read the menu? I always say a dry martini slips down a treat on these winter evenings!" — "Champagne? Why not?!" But it was not to be. Far from delighting the punters with winning ways and radiant smiles, I have never been able to manage much more than a rictus grin-grimace as I stagger from one fuck-up to the next, tripping over my own feet, forgetting my biro, exuding incompetence from every pore. I am a bleeding disaster of a waiter and shall leave Patrick's employ just as soon as I can line up something else of a part-time nature.

Now, there are only four sorts of punters who go to Van Rijn's, and they are as follows (NB: all punters come in pairs):

1) two same-sexers in love (or at least, giving it a go), on for a romantic evening far from the harsh realities of Thatcher's Victorian Britain;

2) the Punter and the Rentboy;

3) the straight couple who have come for a few laughs;

4) the straight couple who have strayed in off the street and

haven't noticed anything odd.

Of these four categories I have always found the Punter-and-Rentboy to be the most intrinsically terrifying. Because I never cotton on! I have to have my *nose rubbed in it* before I can see the appalling truth. My trouble is, of course, I'm too trusting. I take people at face value. Always have.

Scenario: it is late. The last customers have just left. I have locked the front door, emptied the bins and put bleach in the loos. I am standing halfway down the back stairs, changing back into my jeans and T-shirt (there's nowhere else to change). Patrick is standing at the top of the stairs in the small kitchen where we keep the butter and stuff, pretending to do the accounts but actually burning holes into my skinny buttocks with his red laser-eyes. He is crooning something about how well I did tonight, and how I seem to be picking up the little skills of waiting with remarkable speed. I know full well that he is lying through his yellowing teeth. I spilt a glass of iced water all over a rentboy's lap (probably just what he needed, come to think of it), gave a woman a gin-and-tonic with no gin in it, forgot orders. My heart sinks within me as I feebly attempt to forecast what it will be like when Patrick twigs that I have no intention of rendering up my ass to his loathed caresses.

"I like your jeans!" he chirps, fake-casually. We are obviously in the realms of sophisticated verbal fireworks here.

"Yes, they're . . . um . . . um . . ." I reply, too tired to match the sheer sparkle of his dialogue, "jeans."

I whop on my trainers and letterman's jacket and hot-foot it down the stairs and through the kitchen.

"Bye, Bibi!"

"Bye, Lenny! Sleep well!"

I step out into the cold air. Suddenly I realize that Bibi (straight straight STRAIGHT) has just gone out of his way to be friendly. The way he said "Sleep well". My head spins. I can think of no appropriate way to react. The thought that he's straight and beautiful and likes me and I don't hate him for being straight gives me a buzz you could land a jet on. I love Bibi and it doesn't matter. I leap down the road at a level of exactly two inches above the ground at all times.

The last tube is long gone and I have to wait for a nightbus. But the time canters by as my head continues to spin with newly de-traumatized love of Bibi. I get home.

Now, when I tell you that there are two sinks in our kitchen — two sinks! — you will probably be jealous. Little do you know. The fact that there are two sinks just means that there is always twice as much washing up that hasn't been done. Not only are there two sinks, there's also lots of room generally. We live in a luxuriously big house, but for reasons complicated enough to threaten to entirely overwhelm my narrative if touched upon more than fleetingly, this wonderful spaciousness tends to weigh down upon us in the form of a heavy burden rather than constitute a source of fun and freedom from care. It just seems that the more space you have the more dirt you can have, and the more decorating there needs to be done. There is now so much decorating that needs to be done that the very thought of the task that theoretically lies ahead is enough to send any of us screaming for the nearest supply of marijuana. Somehow you can tell it's not going to happen. It is all we can do to prevent the place from turning into a complete pig-sty. Elegant living will have to wait.

When I get back, both the sinks are full of washing up. It's late and I'm tired. All I want is a bowl and a spoon. All I want is some yoghurt and a little chopped fruit "before retiring" — is that so much to ask? I find myself engulfed by a flood of self-pity. Things look black indeed. I walk out of the kitchen into the sitting room. I cannot face plunging my hand into the foul and greasy cold waters in the sinks to extract a bowl. I sit down and pick up a copy of the *New Internationalist*. But my heart is not in it. I get up and go into the kitchen again. I remember that *one of the sinks has a plug that is still attached to its chain*. We're laughing! I pull the plug out and watch the greasy tide withdraw. We're doing fine. I find a bowl and gingerly fish it out of the wreckage. I wash it and dry it. I look for a spoon. Cutlery lies around in the bottom of the sink in foetid pools. I notice that Bjorn has left a soggy teabag in the sink. That pesky Swede! My frustration knows no bounds. For some reason I cannot help feeling this is the height of sluttiness. *Unhigurnic* indeed! My blood boils. Swaying with fatigue, I fish the soggy teabag out of the strewn cutlery. As I pick it up I become horridly aware that the teabag seems to be strangely heavy, lumpy . . . that it has little paws and a mouth and a little pink tail . . . I let out a terrified yelp and drop what is in my hand, springing back. I have been holding a dead mouse!

Suddenly the kitchen is full of people: Eric, Tookie, Bjorn, and some people who I've never met before in my life, but who seem to live here as they are in their pyjamas. Apparently I have been screaming the place down.

When Bjorn learns the horrid truth he is most upset. "No," he pronounces firmly. "This is *extremely unhigurnic*. This dead mouse is not good. I cannot live in a house with dead mice."

Tookie reels about the room, sickened and harrowed, "grossed out".

Only Eric, like a knight in shining armour, is evolved enough to pick the dead mouse up, wrap it in newspaper and take it to the outside bin, thus delivering us all from our waking nightmare.

SIX

Don't dream it – do it – that's Corey's philosophy, and how wise it is! While the rest of us are sitting listlessly at home, *dreaming* of being screwed standing up while handcuffed to a tree, Corey is actually out there in the real world (on Hampstead Heath to be exact) getting on with it.

The marvellous thing is, he's quite prepared to talk about it. Come to think of it, it's hard to stop him. Eric and I will meet him for lunch in the First Out or Pollo's maybe, and he will *attempt* to stagger in, *attempting* to look all tired and tousled (actually he never looks tired, never has black rings under his eyes, which are forever bright and twinkling like two shiny little pebbles washed by the sea) and let it slip – by the by – that he *hasn't had much sleep*.

"Oh?" we will enquire; "Not sleeping well?"

"No, no," says he, as if not very interested in the conversation, "I just got to bed rather late, that's all. 3am."

The menu will be perused for a little while, and then one of us will venture, "Oh really?" as if hardly paying attention.

"Yes – out late," he will announce crisply. "What's the pesto like here?"

"Out late?" says myself or Eric; "hitting the clubs, eh?"

"Nah," says he, very bored-sounding by this stage, as if he

really wants to get onto some other more interesting topic, "I was *up on the Heath.*"

"Oh — *up on the Heath* . . ." we reply, as if bored out of our skulls; and the conversation draws, disappointingly, to a close. It is quite evident that Corey's night out on the Heath has been more exciting than the combined nights of every single scaredy-cat same-sexer in London who *merely hung around in bars* or — worse still — *merely went round to a friend's house for dinner and a few laughs*. I for one would give my entire plate of pesto to know what Corey did on the Heath last night, but of course it isn't really etiquette to ask.

I remember when we first met (of which more later — no, I *haven't forgotten*) and the subject of the Heath came up, I must have betrayed my lack of sophistication in a way that made it obvious from the outside — maybe my eyes popped out of my head or something — for I remember Corey saying brightly, "Oh, don't you go to the Heath?"

"Um . . . no," I mumbled stupidly, cursing my provincial upbringing.

"A lot of people aren't into it," said he philosophically. "You either are or you aren't, I think. I must say that, looking back on it, I honestly think the best sex I've had has been on the Heath. No shilly-shallying about, no cooking breakfast the next morning, just up there — get on with it — home and bed."

"Yes, I can see that," I muttered. "It must be very ... very ..." But no adjective came.

"Oh but you must know how it is," he went on, by now more or less unstoppable, "when you've been out for a curry and then you nip into a bar and bring home a bit of trade — " (*trade? trade?*) " — the sex always seems to be . . . I dunno . . . all elbows in your neck and things — don't you think?"

I nodded wisely. "Oh — absolutely — damn elbows . . ."

I went away from this conversation very confused. Firstly, I had to find out what *trade* was. I found out, but I still didn't understand. I was frankly baffled (still am) by Corey's apparent ability to walk into a same-sexer bar — any same-sexer bar — snap his fingers at the stud of his choice and take him straight back home and into his bedroom in very much the same fashion as he had previously (one imagines) ordered his curry.

47

Now, it is my personal theory that this positively poetic philosophy of Corey's — *don't dream it, do it* — has, by a curious paradoxical twist of fate, actually had a negative affect on Eric's karma. I've never told him as much, but it has been niggling at the back of my mind for some time now. You see, if you're a don't-dream-it-do-it man, you don't really have much time for the magical make-believe world of the stage and the screen (silver or small). Why don't you? Because you're out there getting on with it, that's why! You don't need to imagine alternative worlds of glamour and excitement if your own life is positively groaning with sensual gratification. You just don't care. Sometimes Eric and I will be really hot to see some fab new movie with exploding heads in it and stuff, and we'll ring up Corey and say *Howzaboutit, Corey old chap*? and he'll hum and ha and eventually say something like, Well, I *might* meet you there but I must say I don't much fancy the idea of being cooped up in a cinema for two hours. Which, being translated into the vernacular, means: I yearn for the wide-open spaces, and in particular, Hampstead Heath. Corey can be rather disparaging about theatre too, which I must say I think is a little insensitive as he knows perfectly well Eric is an actor at rest. The last time we all went to see a play together it was a thing at the Bush, which is just a room above a pub really, and Corey kicked up a hell of a fuss over the price of the tickets (a slightly unexpected £7). "What a farce!" he cries, "paying £7 to sit in some poxy upstairs room watching a load of poncy middle-class southerners pretending to be exploited Glaswegians who haven't got the price of a bus-fare home!" He *did* have a point in a way, but he was also missing a much more important point (almost too obvious to mention) namely that if a society loses its ART, then what, oh what, is going to become of its SOUL? Eric went very quiet at this point, and it is my belief that he was just a teensy weensy bit put out. I think he had actually rather enjoyed the whole evening up to that moment, feeling that it offered fresh hope for actors at rest everywhere.

And Corey's absolutely horrid about Barbara Honigsbaum. Now, it's true that she is just a tad snotty, and it *was* rather funny when she stepped on the slug, but I think it's important to get things in perspective. Barbara Honigsbaum is not the Antichrist, just another ordinary kid who wants to live forever, immortalised by fame. Is that such a crime? Things have been rather tense lately if the truth be told, as Barbara has been round at our place rather a lot, getting help from Tookie with her new role, and Corey (who, let's face it, *doesn't actually live in the house*) has been radiating bad vibes all the time she's there. Luckily she is too thick-skinned to notice, and Corey's cruel jibes have until now proved to be water off a duck's back. But still. Barbara is in this play (written specially for her I think) which is going to be quite wild, about a mother who has a son who was in an accident — all this happens in the Deep South of course, as all good plays should — and she hires this man who's just come out of prison (where he was doing time for MURDER!) to look after her invalid son. All three become inexorably entangled in a triangle of desire!! Barbara is always round by the time I come down for my breakfast (late-ish), swishing around the sitting-room saying things like, "Life is very hard, Mr de Lakes — you see in me a broken woman!" and she usually stays right through to late-night camomile-tea-time too.

Bjorn, of course, being a crusty sod at the best of times, resents her presence as much as Corey does, but none of us takes much notice of what he thinks. His voice has this indescribable barking quality which just makes you want to take him by the neck and put him out of his misery without further ado. I know I shouldn't say this, but Bjorn is obviously *really stupid*. He has this ridiculous job selling overpriced trinkets or something in some hotel lobby, and he can't even do that right. He comes home with stories of how he made out a Masterchage slip and then gave *all three* pages to the customer, thus losing the shop eighty quid at one fell Scandinavian swoop. He says it only happens because his "psychic energy" is "low", and this, of course, can be traced directly back to the trauma of knowing that there are mice and infested hazelnuts in his domestic environment. Maybe it's also connected to the dog shit on the sofa, for that matter — but let that rest. The point is, *we warned him* when he originally moved in (all smiles and politeness then, ha ha) that he was coming to live in what was in some ways the intellectual centre of London and certainly a thriving community of highly creative mavericks, and if he couldn't stand the heat then he was strongly advised to stay out of the kitchen. He smiled and smiled and gave us all little presents and said he was the most tolerant person in the world and what's more he actually *throve* (I remember him using the word) on being surrounded by creative energy. Throve indeed. You should hear the fuss when I'm rehearsing with Kenny! (Kenny and I have a band — a sort of synth-duo. I write all the words and sort of talk, and Kenny does all the music. We don't really have a singer. We were going to be called *Lenny and Kenny*, but that sounded too soft, so now we're just called *Queer*, which is harder and more challenging.)

Shall I tell you what *really* gets me about that Bjorn? Well, I told you he has this thing that one day he's going to be a famous advertising executive, didn't I? How he squares this with his dogged insistence that he puts karma above all else in his priorities I do not know. But anyway, he's obviously dipped into some absurd paperback about psychology or something, because he has a habit of sitting curled up in front of the TV, shoes on, barking fatuous comments about the quality of the ads that come up: "Yes, this is a very good advertisement. Shall I explain why?" — or (garrottes at the ready, boys) "*Do you understand why?*" Do we understand indeed! There we will be, settling in nicely to some fab screen gem, only to be jolted rudely back to reality every time the ads come up by a mad, yapping voice haranguing us about whether or not we have understood why something is good or not.

Classic case: Ad comes on, willowy girlie in fab make-up drifts about a room. The room is *completely white*. The product is paint or something, up-market stuff. Suddenly a voice which sounds like someone being sick makes you jump out of your skin: "No. This is not good. *Shall I explain why?*"

Silence. Thought-bubbles come out of our heads: "No, Bjorn, no need, just shut the fuck up."

"I'll explain. My studies in this area of psychology have revealed to me that the concept of a *white room* is intrinsically terrifying. This is a universal response. All human beings are terrified by white rooms. I can't believe the people who made this ad didn't know this. They are actually *putting people off* the product. Can you believe anyone could be so stupid?"

My tone is mild but firm. "I rather like white rooms," I

announce, "which I suppose you could say puts a bit of a damper on your fascinating theory."

"Hm," he says; "I'm not so sure."

Later on the ad returns. Willowy girlie, fab make-up, white room. Suddenly we are alarmed by a strange moaning noise coming from the direction of our once-rather-nice sofa. "Ooh ... ooh ... I'm so ... *frightened* ..."

He'll have to go.

SEVEN

I can honestly and sincerely say, with my hand on my heart, that there is nothing in the world I find so pathetic as someone who likes to give offence *purely for the sake of giving offence*. Frankly I think it's the sort of thing that you should grow out of when your acne clears up (if it clears up), and if you still haven't got it out of your system by the time that happy day comes round, then I just feel very sorry for you. I really do.

Unfortunately, though, the world of the same-sexer is fraught with moral dilemmas — they are in fact our bread and butter — and I can see one careering towards me even as we speak, at a hundred mph, snorting flames from its nostrils and greedily licking its chops. My problem is that it is of absolute necessity to the telling of the tale of *how I lost that which can never be regained* that I touch upon certain — how shall I put it? — *hard realities* of same-sexer life. Certain throbbing realities. I have thought and thought and thought, but have been able to find absolutely no way round the problem. I have meditated. I have burnt incense. I have — don't laugh — consulted a non-corporeal being with whom I sometimes commune when I am scaling the steep cliff-faces of enlightenment. But the problem has remained.

After an extended period of soul-searching I have been forced to a conclusion, and it is this: you either tell a story or you don't, and at the end of the day there really can be no half-measures. I am working on the assumption, of course, that those to whom I am speaking are listening on a purely voluntary basis (that my words have not, for example, received the dubious honour of being set as an O-level text) and that, this being the case, no one will be able to accuse me of roughly raping their intellectual virginity. I would remind my listeners that we live in a free country (ha ha), and that they are at liberty to part company with this little same-sexer and his wicked words at any such time as they may hear the clarion call of Decency sounding crisp and shrill, or feel the very natural urge to bury their heads in the Sands of Unknowing.

Having made this disclaimer, I trust I may now speak with complete candour.

Which of us can deny that the sexual act, in all its forms, is a strange and wonderful thing, an endless source of surprises? — that the human body is a complex instrument upon which many play but few make music? And which of us would be so naive as to assert that *experience does not pay*? Poets through the ages have sung (more or less tunefully) of the eternal opposition of the twin principles of innocence and expertise — as equal and opposite as night and day! — and which of us has not paused awhile, at some stage during his or her terrestrial life, while in the heat of the act itself perhaps, or maybe during the golden, mellow moments of its recollection, teased and perplexed by the question of *just how experienced or innocent would we really like to be*? The less evolved among us will no doubt hark nostalgically back to days of childhood, before the forbidden fruit was first taken upon the tongue, before the harsh geometry of limbs, fingers, noses and orifices came between us and our ideal dreams of the marriage of true minds; the more evolved, meanwhile, will surge ever fearlessly onwards like voyagers on unchartered seas, doggedly experimental and daily growing in the sophistication of their palates. Sometimes it seems to me that we are like two tribes — and I do not mean the tribes of Male and Female, nor of Same-Sexer and his more biologically productive counterpart, — I mean the two tribes of the Timid and the Brave, the Lions and the Lambs. *There*, to be sure, lies the great divide!

Corey, for example, belongs to the Lion tribe — as I was to find out to my (ecstatic) cost that fateful morning when I rang the bell of the house in which I now live, dressed in my Sunday best with the trusty Barney at my side.

"Hello we're from the local church and were just wondering whether you were interested in Father God or Christ Jesus at all and whether you might like to invite them into your life at all and if not whether you might like to talk about it at all and if not *why not* and if not not NOT, then is there anyone else in the house who you think *might* be interested in Father God or Christ Jesus . . . at all?"

Now, for most of us, those funny pictures you see in mystical oriental sex manuals are at best only indirectly applicable to our lives, like the plastic models of molecules which once decorated one's school's science laboratory; but Corey has always been a man to take his pleasure in deadly earnest. Where others of us have been tinkering with (say) classic old motorbikes in an attempt to get the best possible performance out of them, Corey has always devoted his spare time to mastering the mechanics of the carnal. So it should come as no surprise to you when I say that Corey *knows what he likes*. Actually his taste in the realm of the senses is catholic, but there some things for which he really will drop everything — which he will go out of his way to, um, set up.

There is one thing in particular.

I have never shared this with Eric, but I have a secret theory that the kitchen table in our house — marvellous big old oaken affair — has a special place in Corey's heart. I have given the matter careful thought and correlated the data at my disposal with monk-like thoroughness. Two things I can present as incontrovertible fact:

1) The surface of our kitchen table is exactly thirty inches (760mm) from the ground.

2) Corey is exactly six feet tall.

Less incontrovertibly, but still pretty damn interestingly:

3) If Leonardo da Vinci is to be believed, a man's *hard reality* is to be found *at the exact mid-point* of his anatomy.

Conclusion: all the evidence points towards the sobering consideration that we have a kitchen table-top which is a convenient (not to say ideal) six inches lower than Corey's *hard reality*.

Lambs will no doubt be quite baffled by all this, but *Lions* will know exactly what I am talking about, and furthermore will all agree that if we're talking table-tops, that six-inch figure really isn't negotiable by much more than an inch either way. I have been round to Corey's place (it's in Ladbroke Grove) and once, when no one was in the room, I whipped out my tape measure and got the vital statistics on the rather horrid formica-topped monstrosity he's got in his kitchen. Just as I thought. Thirty-three inches. Corey would have to wear high heels or stand on a box to get any use out of that thing, and as we all know, no one wants to have to worry about balance when scaling the steep cliff-faces of satisfaction.

You're probably wondering, after all my stories, how Corey and Eric manage to make it *work*, this open relationship of theirs. I know I used to. Well, the answer is this. They have a *manifesto*. At least, they have this bit of paper with all the rules of the relationship set out on it, and the word "MANIFESTO" written at the top. I have a sneaking suspicion that "manifesto" is not the precise word for the meaning they had in mind, but of course I wouldn't dream of saying so. This is what the document says:

MANIFESTO:

1) Eric and Corey are in love, and promise to stay in love with each other until the end of time.

2) Having eschewed all the useless role-models so oppressively foisted upon them by the heterosexual patriarchy, and in particular the outrageous concept of monogamy, Eric and Corey have wisely decided to have an *open relationship*.

This means they can both fuck about as much as they like.

3) Being, however, sensitive to each other's emotional needs and also desirous to preserve each other in an ongoing state of health, they have wisely agreed upon the following simple and easy-to-remember rules with regard to said fucking around:

    a) Neither party shall engage in carnal relations with any third party *who is already known to the other party*.

    b) Neither party shall engage in carnal relations with any third party *more than once*.

    c) Whenever either party engages in carnal relations with

a third party, he must make a full and exhaustive report of the whole thing to the other party.

d) Should either party, in course of having carnal relations with a third party, scale the particular steep cliff-face of satisfaction so crudely dubbed "penetrative" by the heterosexual patriarchy, he shall protect the ongoing health of all three parties by insisting upon the use of a condom. No excuses please.

e) Both parties must *own up* if they get crabs.

This "manifesto" is glued to the inside of the door of Eric's bedroom cupboard (and there's supposedly a xerox of it in Corey's room too, though I must say I've never noticed it). The idea is that when he's got some bit of "trade" into his room (the inevitable chaser to a curry and couple of pints) he will open the cupboard in search of KY or handcuffs or something and the manifesto will LEAP out at him. Actually Eric never does take bits of trade back to his room after he goes out for curry, but the point is, *it would be there if he did.*

Sometimes Eric's failure to be unfaithful to Corey seems to be as much of an embarrassment as my failure to find myself a husband (though I, of course, have more excuse, with my spring lamb looks and my sometimes glued-on beard). In many ways we make a right pair when we go out on the town, as we sometimes do when the moon is full, all dressed up and soaked in supposedly irresistible fragrances. Eric's usual serenity goes out of the window when it comes to dressing for the bars.

"But *can I wear yellow*?" he will say; "can I *really* wear yellow?"

He has put on a stunning long-sleeved vest thing in radiant buttercup yellow with buttons part of the way down the front. He looks fucking fab in it. He tucks it into his raunchy 501s. I know they are raunchy because Pete, the guy in American Classics, told us they were.

"You look fucking fab," I tell him. "If you weren't my flatmate I'd go down on you, here and now."

Sophisticated banter.

"I dunno," says he, wrinkling his nose. "If I wear the green-and-yellow letterman's jacket I'll look coordinated, and if there's one thing I can't stand it's men in coordinated clothes."

I sigh patiently. "Yellow suits you. Green suits you," I explain, as if talking to a three-year-old. "Maybe if the stuff came from *Top Man* you might look co-ordinated, but it's different with classic old stuff. Now stop whinging and can we please hit the town?"

"But I look like I'm on my way to the fucking Roof Gardens!" he bleats.

"So wear the semi-see-through black airtex T-shirt!" I cry, exasperated beyond words. "What are we anyway, old ladies?"

The fact of the matter, as we both very well know, is that Eric's shapely figure will push out in all the right places regardless of the colour of his clothes, and for this reason I have only a limited amount of time for his endless stream of self-doubt.

The plan is to meet a couple of old friends of Eric's from California who are in town for a week, and take them somewhere exciting and maybe even a tad sleazy. They are a straight couple, you see, and Eric and I have a theory that in some ways straight people are just as desperate to escape the oppression of the patriarchy as we are. We are meeting them in a pub off Leicester Square. On the way we have a gander at *Capital Gay* and after a lot of extremely careful deliberation decide to take them down the Phoenix to see one of our favourite strippers. (This is a man called Rick. He dresses up as a construction worker and his act is actually rather artistic. He's a psychology student you see — straight — married! — and he also has a body which makes your mouth go very dry whenever you look at it. Maybe I shouldn't tell you this, but *even though he's straight and married* he sometimes does shows at private same-sexer parties, and, if the foul beast Rumour is to be believed, he even does the whole Baby Oil thing and encourages members of his own sex to come into direct contact with his own very hard reality! But I'm sure you don't want to hear about all this.)

We pick up Roy and Naomi and hit the Phoenix with high hopes of a truly challenging evening.

The Phoenix turns out to be a lot seedier than either of us remembered it as being, and we suddenly feel rather embarrassed. Here we are with these nice friendly Americans who want to see the sights of swinging London and we've taken them to a dingy underlit cellar which looks like some hellish students' union bar, where everyone is sitting round with a lean and hungry look waiting for a guy to take his dick out. Rick's act is a bitter disappointment (they all go off in the end, strippers) and all in all the evening is a complete failure.

Just as we are about to leave, Eric bumps into Corey. Hideous embarrassment. We all stand round like Noel Coward characters, introducing each other. Thankfully the lighting is too dim to reveal our hot blushes. I suppose in many ways you could say it's a prime example of human psychology, really, the fact that, even though Eric and Corey have a written manifesto setting out the exact terms of their marvellous relationship, and even though they are both blissfully happy with the set-up in general, it is always somehow excruciatingly embarrassing when they accidentally bump into each other in the context of some cheap pick-up joint.

EIGHT

We get back home and, after an insipid cup of Sleepytime Herbal Infusion, trudge wearily up to our respective rooms. I get to my room and there's a note on the door:

STOP! DON'T GO INTO YOUR ROOM!
Dear Lenny – this is just in case you do come home tonight after all (Bjorn assured me that you are staying at Kenny's). I have given Barbara your room. The poor thing was so wound up about her part that I really didn't want her going home alone. Quite honestly I really thought she might <u>do something stupid.</u> I know you'll understand.
   – Tookie.

I am beside myself with rage. Where Bjorn got the absurd idea that I was staying at Kenny's tonight I cannot imagine. It does seem to me that if he's going to eavesdrop on other people's conversations (I sure as hell didn't say anything to *him* about my movements) he should at least master the English language first.

I go into Eric's room and stomp about crossly, cursing the pesky Swede and the land that so unwisely gave him birth. Eric tells me to shut up and sit down while he rolls me a joint, which we both probably need after the disasters of the evening. Soon the drug starts to take hold and my troubles seem infinitely less real. We both agree, however, that the house has become more or less intolerable and the only thing for it is to go to Brighton for a while and lie low. We decide to make all the necessary arrangements first thing in the morning.

Just as I am beginning to feel quite exceptionally mellow I remember I haven't got a bed to sleep in and I am engulfed by a fresh wave of outrage. Eric generously lets me share his futon on the condition that I stop whinging without further ado. I know which side my bread is buttered on, and wisely obey.

In the morning we phone an old actor friend of Eric's called Roly who's moved to Brighton with his wife and baby and ask him if we can stay the night at his place. Roly says yes, but there isn't much room and they sort of have their hands full what with the new baby and everything. It is still only two months old and Roly's wife Christine is very tired. Eric promises that we won't be any trouble and we just want to stay one night, and the whole thing is fixed. Eric and I both happen to have three days off in a row and our plan is to go down on Thursday night and see if we can charm Roly and his wife into extending their kind invitation to include Friday and Saturday night as well. It's a bit naughty but sometimes there's no other way.

I get to work and say hi to Bibi. Fifty-five minutes and counting to Zero "T-shirt-off" Hour. We chat of this and that for about ten seconds, during which time an eternity passes and I drown in the pools of his fantastic dark brown eyes. Palm trees sway and camels doze. Far away I hear the distant sound of his words . . . something about being a student . . . special visa to study in London for ten months . . . I nod as if listening while my mind explodes into a zillion brightly-coloured splinters. I realize that I must still be stoned from last night and I decide it might be prudent to pull myself together before I start unbuttoning his fly.

"How fascinating!" I chirp; "You must tell me more about yourself over a pint and a curry some day . . ." The mention of curry has the unfortunate effect of reminding me of Corey picking up trade, and for a blinding split-second I am guiding Bibi into my bedroom with a light but intimate pat on his compact yet yielding arse. Twelve gallons of adrenalin shoot into my bloodstream. His eyes are skittish from drink; his teeth flash like beacons as he throws me a knowing smile. My Buddha-lamp is on, casting soft shadows, and the divine Wolfgang Amadeus is leading a chugging string-section through a never-ending slow movement, choked with memories of Eden and all its fruits. And then in a swift, elegant motion that I already know so well he pulls his T-shirt up over his head, filling my field of vision with velvety brown skin and an undulating landscape of muscle. "Here," I mutter, boldly addressing myself to the task of unclothing him further, "let me help you off with these..." I fumble with his belt and then ease his jeans and boxers over the lazy (baroque?) curve of his sun-fried butt. Hot spicy breath on my cheeks as I...

The reverie fades. I am cleaning one of the lavatories. I vaguely remember coming home from work last time and having made some sort of breakthrough about not caring that I was in love with Bibi. I try to remember why I didn't care but I can't. The thought is absurd. Naturally the whole business is driving me out of my mind. I resolve to get a new job just as soon as soon can be.

Six o'clock approaches and I return the bleach to the kitchen, accidentally-on-purpose wedging the door open. So far so good. I get the bar-cleaning stuff and position myself carefully. Two minutes and counting. Bibi has got his vegetables soaking and is casting an critical eye over the work surfaces. Soon now, soon now.

Suddenly "Patricia" (who, as you will remember, is in fact a member of the male sex) comes bolting down the stairs, blond tresses flying, with the information that it's Wednesday and have I forgotten that we have to polish all the mirrors on Wednesday and I had better look snappy about it because Patrick will be here any minute and he is *really funny* about mirrors. I curse. I consider skipping the mirrors but remember what happened last time and shudder. I take some Windolene round to the far side of the bar where the big mirrors are and soon they are so clean I can see my face in them. I rush back to my former position, only to find that Bibi is now wearing a new T-shirt and the moment has passed. I curse a thousand curses. But there is worse to come.

Over dinner (a meal enjoyed together by waiting and kitchen staff, only, alas, always at separate tables) I glean the horrific news that there is to be a Christmas cabaret at the restaurant in which all staff are expected to make an appearance. Members of staff with good muscular development will just wear G-strings while those whose beauty lies primarily from the neck upwards will be required to parade in drag. My heart sinks. It goes without saying, of course, that I won't make it into the G-string category, not even if I work out every day for the next two weeks. I have always had an absolute horror of wearing women's clothing and the thought of doing so on a tawdry makeshift stage under the impertinent gaze of forty paying punters fills me with an irrational sense of panic. I casually mention to Patrick, when I get a moment, that I will unfortunately *not* be appearing in the Christmas cabaret, but he just smiles sourly and informs me that the cabaret is an ancient tradition of Van Rijn's and surely I must have known about it when I took the job. His tone leaves me in absolutely no doubt that I shall be out on my arse if I decline to pad my tits, and I go back to my waiting in a state of confusion and nausea.

A rentboy on Table 12 asks me in mock politeness what the liver-and-duck's-meat starter is.

"Well, it's . . . um . . . liver and duck's meat," I reply stupidly. He looks up at me with superior amusement. This is all I need.

"Yes, but exactly how is it cooked?" he insists.

I haven't got the faintest idea how it is cooked. "It's . . . um . . . fried," I tell him. But I know I'm not getting away with it. He's got me on the run, and he knows it. Why can't I be like Kate and Patricia? They would probably just laugh and say something really cheeky like *What does it matter how it's cooked, you little tart, it'll all be the same when it comes out the other end*! And everyone would have a good old laugh. But of course I'm me, and that means I am doomed to be forever singled out for special humiliation by upitty male prostitutes.

"Yes, but before it's fried," he insists, "how is it prepared?"

I rack my brains. I have in fact seen the stuff before it's fried. There's this big bowl of it in the kitchen. It's just basically lumpy red stuff, all sort of slimy and foul-looking. I have no idea what they have done to it, nor even what part of the duck it represents.

"You know, it's quite right of you to give me a hard time about it," I attempt to chirp but only mutter, with a hideous rictus grimace which by the same token was intended as a winning smile; "and you know what? I think I'll go straight to the kitchen and get the low-down from Chef himself!"

But by now the little fucker has the bit between his teeth. "No, I just want to know how it's prepared," says he, raising his voice. "You obviously don't know, do you?"

I consider pointing out that I may not know how the liver-and-duck-meat starter is prepared, but at least I'm not going to have to sit on my employer's willy before the night is out. I wisely bite back what would have been, I think, very much the last word in the argument and retire from the field of battle.

On my way down to the kitchen I remember that Chef is Japanese and I can't understand a word he says. I decide to ask Bibi. He is very helpful and also wonderfully sympathetic when I tell him about how horrid the rent boy is being.

"Tell him to come down and sort it out with me," he grins radiantly; "tell him Bibi give him a — " (he makes an elegant pelvic thrust gesture) " — he won't forget in a hurry." We have a good old laugh and I remember why it was that I didn't mind being in love with him. He is so relaxed, especially about sex, and I must say I can be so up-tight sometimes. You could almost imagine that, even though he is straight, he might easily stretch a point some day just by way of being a good mate. (Don't think about it! Don't think about it!) Halfway up the stairs on my way back to be further taunted by a no doubt justifiably embittered sex-slave, I remember very clearly how Bibi's whole body came vibrantly alive when he did the pelvic thrust gesture — how it lit up, so to speak, like a Christmas tree — and I am in Arabia again. We are in a tent hung with rich tapestries and I am a sheik or something, puffing imperiously on a hubble-bubble and toying with an exotic sweet-meat. Bibi, naked except for a skimpy toga made of transparent muslin and a turban perhaps and lots of heavy strings of pearls hanging round his neck, dances to the sound of primitive instruments. He is my slave. I can do with him as I please. The frank inadequacy of his toga to conceal the purposeful metamorphosis taking place at his mid-point is making my head spin. I impetuously dismiss all my other slaves with a barked command and an irritable flick of my bejewelled paw. The music stops. For a moment we glower suspiciously at each other, master and servant united in a slavery to passion's more primal behests. "You realize, I suppose, that I could have you killed — just like that — if the whim so took me?" I enquire with a cruel sneer. But my words seem only to inflame him further. Suddenly he is upon me, clawing at my expensive robes and muttering something about . . . um . . . love . . .

"Chef says it's all cut up into strips and marinated in garlic and olive oil, then fried, then served on a bed of lettuce," I pronounce crisply.

"Actually I don't like liver anyway," says the harlot; "I just thought you ought to know what was on the menu. It was the principle of the thing really."

As I walk to the bus stop and go over the humiliations of the evening, I resolve to hand in my notice the very next time I see my loathed employer.

NINE

"I suppose Bjorn *is* rather fun in many ways," I muse, playing with my herb teabag; "but I must say I'm beginning to think he really will have to go."

Eric and I are sitting in the First Out cafe bantering of this and that while keeping a wary eye open for an opportunity for me to find a husband or him to fulfil his onerous infidelity duties.

"I think what I find hardest to take on board is the way he sounds like he's being sick whenever he says anything," I continue. "I *know* it's just because he's Swedish, and I *know* he can't help it, and I really am a teensy bit worried that I might be acquiring some bad karma, but I just can't help it. Whenever he's in the house I feel a strong urge to invest in a pair of earplugs."

Eric chuckles tolerantly but I know he agrees. "By far the best course of action is to have a think about it when we're in Brighton," he says. "Things always seem different in Brighton."

I am struck — as I so often am — by the wisdom of his words. "That's very true — I'd never noticed it before, but blow me down if it isn't God's own truth!" I cry.

Eric and I have only been to two places (discounting my home town — more of a condition than a place): London and Brighton. It's not that we have narrow horizons; we don't (in fact we like to get out the old World Atlas on quiet, stay-at-home evenings, and have a carefully worked-out plan to go to Los Angeles one day in the very near future, just as soon as we can swing the financial side) but that's just how our lives have worked out. And for this reason our thinking, when it comes to the geographic, tends to be rather black-and-white. You're either in London or you're not, and when you're not, you're in Brighton (or the London-to-Brighton train I suppose, but that's just nit-picking).

"It's like before and after sex," says my flatmate.

I nod again, playing with my teabag, then realize that he has entirely lost me. "What's like before and after sex?" I ask, fearful that my mentor may be having some sort of lapse.

"Well, you know what they say . . ." says he.

"No, actually, I don't," I snap impatiently.

Eric lets one of his tolerant sighs escape him. "Things look different before and after sex," he explains, as if addressing a six-year-old.

"Do they?" I am amazed.

Another sigh. "After orgasm a man experiences a mood change," Eric goes on. "You have had an orgasm, haven't you?"

"More than you've had hot dinners," I snap again. "Get to the point."

"Well, they say that if you have a problem and you want to give it full and careful consideration, you should think about it immediately *before* having sex with someone, and then have another think about it immediately *after*. That way you'll see it from a sort of all-round perspective."

"Two questions:" (I reply) "Firstly, would a hand shandy work if you didn't have a boyfriend? and secondly, what has all this got to do with going to Brighton?"

Eric's tone is wise, serene, forgiving of my crabbiness (what a friend!): "In answer to your first, I would say *maybe*. There are hand shandies and hand shandies. Most hand shandies don't really come anywhere near the real thing in terms of the redirection of the flow of vital energies from chakra to chakra. In answer to your second, the connection is that a problem considered in London may seem very different when pondered on a lungful of the salty air of the San Francisco of the British South Coast."

"The what?"
"Brighton."
"Oh."

"Brighton is the San Francisco of the British South Coast, as you very well know," says Eric. "And that is where we shall consider the slippery problem of the pesky Swede. It'll probably seem all very silly and a lot of fuss about nothing when we get there."

"I'm not so sure," say I. "Do we know whose the hazelnuts are yet?"

"Not yet," says he. "But I have put up a notice over the answering machine suggesting another House Meeting. Everyone in the house has got to write down three dates they can make, in order of preference, and when everyone's done that I'm going to take the notice down and see if we can get everyone into one room at the same time. It's our only hope."

Just at this point a nice-looking young guy (foreign, obviously — German? Dutch? — pray he's not Swedish!) comes down the stairs and sits at a table next to ours. He has a lovely vibe on him and I just sort of like the way he sits down and takes off his jacket and puts down his wallet and map of London and tucks into a high-priced salad. I get the irrational idea into my head that he is in some undefined way *approachable*. We decide to let him settle in a bit before making our move.

I tell Eric the appalling news about the Christmas cabaret.

"I reckon I'd better start looking for another job," I conclude.

"There's a job advertised in *Cap. Gay*," says Eric helpfully.

"Oh yeah?" I am intrigued.

"Assistant Editor for Shafter Press I think. They do all those new mags that are reprinting old Fifties porno."

"Sounds absolutely marvellous."

"Maybe you should apply. But they do say in big letters at the bottom of the ad that they are looking for someone who is *completely comfortable with his or her sexuality*."

"What are you trying to imply?" I demand, hurt, " — that I haven't reached Identity Integration yet?"

"Did I say that?" says he.

"I'll show you how integrated I am!" I declare, and get up and walk over to where the foreign boy is sitting. "Excuse me," I venture, clearing my throat politely; "I notice there is a spare copy of *Capital Gay* on your table. Would you mind at all if I borrowed it? I'm looking for a job, you see."

"Go ahead," he replies, very politely.

I return to our table beaming with triumph. In fact I feel so triumphant that I don't even say anything to rub it in. It is blindingly obvious that, in terms of striking up a relationship with the foreign boy, I am way in the lead. I coolly open *Cap. Gay*.

"There is of course another way of looking at it," says Eric.

"Looking at what?"

"At the whole Christmas cabaret thing," says he.

"I'm just not doing it and that's that," I declare. "I don't want to hear any more about it. What are you trying to do? You want your flatmate to be a drag-queen?"

"I must say I don't really mind what my flatmate is," says he, serene to the last; "however, there is, as I said, another way of looking at it. Didn't you say that *all* the staff are expected to perform?"

"Everyone."

"And that you've either got to wear a G-string or drag, depending on muscularity?"

"Gay Lib is alive and well and living in Fulham," I spit.

"Well, if what you say is true," says my flatmate, with an air of pulling out his ace-card, "then *what do you think Bibi will be wearing?*"

My jaw drops open. "My God — you're right! He'll be in a ..." But the word gets stuck in my throat. *Bibi will be wearing nothing but a G-string.*

"So it seems to me," Eric concludes, "that you are faced with something of a classic dilemma:

1) leave, and have done with the whole damn thing — and, incidentally, probably run out of pocket-money at Christmas and be unable to offer to buy handsome men drinks;

or

2) stay, do the show, have your masculinity insulted in front of forty paying punters, *and get to see Bibi with near as dammit no clothes on.*"

"Shit! Shit! Shit!" I hiss. It looks as if I am going to be doing the cabaret after all. We leave. (Note: I have completely forgotten about the nice foreign boy because I am so cross.)

To get my mind off the whole distressing subject of the cabaret, Eric decides that we should go to his favourite bookshop, which is in Charing Cross Road, and check out what might be new in the way of intellectual stimulation. When we get there we go straight to the gay section where (what a small world!) we bump into Eric's friend Dave, who has just had a book of short stories published. I am terrifically impressed. Dave is obviously far too modest to go in for any sort of self-promotion, but before long we have snaffled out a copy of his fab book, which actually we notice is standing out quite well on the shelf as someone has stacked it with its marvellous cover facing outwards. Eric and I, by now in a frenzy of excitement, both buy a copy and leap out of the shop, scarcely able to believe that one of our friends has been magically transformed — apparently overnight — into a star.

On the tube going home we both read Dave's book. The first story is a mind-blowing tale in which a handsome young skinhead meets a handsome young Tory voter just as morning is breaking over yet another Thatcher election victory. They have sex, but somehow it doesn't "click", and the skinhead ends up giving the snotty guy a good old kick in the teeth. Marvellous stuff! And good to see it on the shelves, too, and to think of guilty Tory-voting same-sexers taking it home in the hope of a cheap thrill or two, only to have their entire value system blown to smithereens in the first ten pages!!

When I have finished the story and pondered awhile on its many hidden meanings, I unfold *Cap. Gay* and peruse the headlines. To my astonishment I find a scribbled message written on the front page in pencil:

Dear Frend,
My name is Mateus and I am coming from Germany. I am arriving in London today and I am looking for a good time. I am looking at you and your big frend who looks like a llama for a long time now, and I hope you will come over and talk to me or maybe ask to borrow this newspaper. When you have read this note, look at me and nod if you fancy me.
Love, Mateus.
PS: I fancy <u>you.</u>

When I have read the message I am so cross that I cannot speak for twenty minutes. We get back and I furiously make myself an organic peanut butter sandwich, even though Tookie told me yesterday that organic peanuts are actually *worse* for you than non-organic peanuts.

TEN

My love of the divine Wolfgang Amadeus and the transmissions from outer space he so faithfully transcribed dates back to the days before my native innocence was not very ceremoniously transformed (in the kitchen of the house in which I now live, and with the indispensable help of the venerable old oaken table there) into a full and ghastly knowingness of good and evil (of which more later). It was in fact the mild and dog-eyed Barney, my church brother, who first got me hooked. We would sit in the nasty room he rented in a house in Acton (Acton!), freaking out without the help of drugs as our guru laid chord-change after chord-change on us till we were fit to have died from an excess of pleasure. Probably a fair amount of corked-up sexual energy was floating about to make all this possible (even seed-spilling was kept to an absolute minimum in those days), but let that rest. The point is, we were transported — to a world where all was sweet and transient and post-baroque, and no matter what happened you knew the big M would always carry you back home and put you to bed (as it were) — in the big, soft, comfortable four-poster bed of that longed-for but oh so teasingly delayed final chord! It was the big M who taught us that *sad* is not necessarily *bad* — and, Lord! the thought has been a great comfort to me as I have grown and blossomed as a humanoid being and temple of the Holy Vibe of the Age of Aquarius. Hopefully that insight will also bear up poor Barney when he sooner or later realizes that he has been conned by the heterosexual patriarchy, but hey! let that rest too. Let all those silly old grumbles and grouches rest in peace. Let us all be very nice to each other and try wherever possible to be friends. Such is my humble philosophy. Take the small example of my father ("example" indeed!) Now, if I was going to be really strict about it I would say the old goat deserves to be whipped from Land's End to John O'Groats for the heinous crime of emotional imperialism (to say nothing of his overriding crime of stupidity) — but no, Forgiveness is now my second name. My PhD in drug-abuse has taught me to have no more truck with a bad vibe than I would with a sabre-toothed tiger, and as far as I am concerned the slate is wiped clean. He can write to me if he wants, he can even call me up on the phone (if that is what he, in the depths of his ignorance, feels is appropriate) and I will tell him all about my challenging new life as a radical maverick, the State of Independence in which I now live, and all the crazy, creative stuff I'm up to. I won't actually *see* him, mind you — I will never see him again as long as I live — but yes, I will banter for a while of this and that without so much as a nod in the direction of the myriad injustices he has heaped upon my poor innocent head. I am in many ways, though young, a very mature person. I have been forced to become mature by the circumstances of my life. In a way I suppose I have grown old before my years — but old in a happy, wise way. (Actually — don't laugh — I was old *before I was born*, which you will find is quite possible if you have a quick flick through *Blinded by the Light*. This is my eightieth life, and that's fairly old in soul-terms. This basic *oldness* of my soul has, I think, been the one thing that has enabled me to get through all the zillion-and-two traumas I have faced, and yet still retain my marvellous optimism and ability to forgive. But I digress.)

Barney's room was not very much larger than the bed that was in it, which for some absurd reason was a double. There was no room for chairs, just a bedside table and an enormous wardrobe, in which he kept his small supply of underwear (of which, believe it or not, more later), his one "casual" outfit (a hideous parody of a lumberjack outfit left over from the late Seventies) and his Sunday best soul-catcher's suit. Barney was like me in that he was a provincial boy at heart; like me had hit the big town in search of he knew not exactly what, and, as was true in my case, the preservation of his virtue had been arranged for by his parents through his enlistment in the ranks of our over-lively church.

Barney's favourite records were Shirley Bassey and Maria Callas, in that order, with the Big M's orchestral miracles limping in—outrageously—in third place. I made it absolutely clear from Day One of our listening partnership that there was to be absolutely no existential warblings from overdressed prima donnas while *I* was in the room, and thus old Wolfy became the main source of our pleasure. Looking back on it, it was perhaps a little naughty of me to call the shots, as I had no record-player of my own; but then presumably he was quite at liberty to plug in for another fix of *Hey Big Spender!* after I had gone home.

I swear you would have thought we were stoned out of our boxes if you had walked in on one of our Big M sessions back in those days. There we would be, stretched out flat on our backs on the gritty sheets of the unmade bed (no chairs), writhing and moaning a little whenever a favourite theme oozed out into the room, rather nasal on Barney's twenty-year-old Dansette but none the less thrilling for that. Come to think of it, we probably *were* pretty high on caffeine. Barney had a very old electric percolator. Sometimes we would make ourselves guilty little meals in his shared kitchen. *I* felt guilty, of course, because my aunt was always very solicitous about feeding me; but though her cooking was more than adequate, the portions she served were invariably just a little too small to satisfy my ravenous nineteen-year-old appetite, and there was usually room for a Vesta Chinese Feast round at Barney's afterwards. Happy days!

I remember I wanted to ask Barney to help me with my application form for the job at the Wholefood Emporium, but I didn't dare. I knew that I was drifting away from the flock by this time, and somehow I couldn't face the thought of his big bloodhound eyes looking at me accusingly. I would simply have to fill in the application on my own and hold my breath till I got a reply.

When Barney and I went to a Pink Floyd gig, he wore his

Seventies lumberjack outfit and I wore a T-shirt which had "JC/DC" on it, in heavy metal lettering, like the AC/DC logo. Underneath were the words: JESUS CHRIST DEMON CRUSHER. Everyone must have thought (correctly) we were mad.

I must say when I look back I do have to have a good old laugh about it. I dread to think what my hair looked like. A little too long, mousy and lank with grease, if my memory serves me right. Now it is crisply bleached and my *trousseau* (my mother always used to call her clothes-collection her *trousseau*), if not exactly the height of fashion, is carefully chosen and quietly challenging. I look terrible in it, but that's beside the point. All clothes look too big on me, even the ones which are too small. I suppose what I really need is dolls' clothes. Eric is terribly rude about about my taste, calling me *Man at C&A* and things, which I must say I find a bit unfair, as he really has an enormous head-start in terms of physical build (which he is always at pains to remind me he didn't even have to work out for). OK, so I *do* buy some of my clothes from C&A, but that is because I am not a snob, and anyway I always wear them *in a subversive way*. At least I don't agonize in front of the bedroom mirror for hours every time I want to nip out to the Royal Oak for a quick half-pint.

This evening Eric has plumped for a "sporty" look — black lycra cycle-shorts topped with a sort of designer rugby shirt and a baseball cap in some unlikely dayglo colour-scheme. The whole ensemble is thrown jauntily out-of-whack by the addition of Eric's extremely old and battered Doctor Martens. Need I add that he looks absolutely fucking fab.

"Can I get away with it?" he is agonizing; "Do I *want* to get away with it?"

I am seated comfortably in a grubby bean-bag pretending to read *Kennedy's Gay Guide to London* and trying not to lose my temper. "Eric," I announce in a tone which betrays the fact that we have been through this scene about a zillion times on previous occasions, "you look absolutely fucking fab. Now can we please go to the Royal Oak before the place crumbles to dust and is one with Nineveh and Tyre?"

Eric turns to me with an exasperated sigh and speaks with a tone of real desperation in his voice: "Lenny, I need your advice. Now will you please stop reading the *Guide* and help me with my look?"

I grumpily let the *Guide* drop to the carpet. "You want me to tell you that if I wasn't your flatmate I'd go down on you? OK. If you weren't my flatmate I'd—"

"I'm serious," he snaps. "Now just tell me one thing: *Can I wear these ridiculous shorts?*"

"What's ridiculous about them?" I reply. "They're black lycra cycle-shorts. They fit you. It's a *frank* look. A bit like wearing nothing on your bum at all. The guys will love you."

"I'm not going in order to pick up men, I'm just nipping out for a drink," he mutters, straining to look at his bum in the mirror.

"Then why all the fuss?" I cry, struggling to get out of the bean-bag.

Big sigh from Eric. "Clothes are not just to attract potential sex partners, as you very well know. Clothes are as much for the wearer as for the onlooker. This is surely one of the first and most easily assimilable messages of Women's Lib, a movement from which we can learn much. Where have you been for the past twenty years?"

"If you're going to be like this all evening I'm not sure I want to drink with you at all," I announce, and slam out of the room.

We go to the Royal Oak. It's not very crowded and it looks sort of different. Then suddenly I realize they've *done it up*!

"My God!" I gasp, "what have they done to the place? Where's the stage?" Now, I have always hated the mind-numbing drag-shows they put on here, but I suppose deep down I must be fundamentally averse to change, for the thought that the stage has gone instantly makes me suspicious. Has there been some sort of conspiracy? Were the police involved? We buy our drinks and check the place out for potential husbands/infidelity opportunities. None present themselves. A black cloud of gloom descends upon us, which we are convinced will never lift.

An hour later the place is really rocking. Droves of alert young men from Putney and Richmond seem to be arriving, intent on wasting their youth and taking life by the scruff of the neck, and drinking it down deeply, and loving it to death! Overstimulation threatens. I mutter a few hoarse words to Eric and go off to the gents to douse myself down with cold water (not enough privacy for the part that needs it most). On my way back I get cruised. *Cruised*! I am beside myself with excitement. It is the first time someone has wanted to sleep with me since — well, since yesterday when Patrick was burning holes in my buttocks with the two red coals that he passes off as eyes. I return the lustful look of my admirer with a shy little doe-like glance and hurry back to Eric. The guy who wants to sleep with me repositions himself so that he can continue to *cruise* me (marvellous word!) while still appearing relatively nonchalant.

"But is he Mr Right?" teases my flatmate.

"Mr Right, as you very well know, does not exist," I remind him, a little narked that he should be bringing up the prickly subject of commitment — or at least steering the conversation in that direction.

"More of a sort of one-night-stand vibe then?" he goes on, still needling me as only he knows how.

I blush hotly in anger and confusion. "One-night stands are very bad for one's karma," I tell him. "It says so in *Blinded by the Light*."

"Actually, it says they *can* be," says he. "It doesn't say they *have* to be. Let's take the thing in its broader context. When was the last time you had sex?"

I pause, calculate. "Six months ago."

"Any good?"

"Not very. The guy had a mental age of six."

"Sounds marvellous! But let that pass. What's your stress level like?"

I pause, calculate. "Stress level: high," I announce. "Work is driving me mad and, apart from anything else, I think Mars is in my third house or something."

"Hm," says he, and sips on his beer. Soon he has come to a conclusion. "My advice is: *take the guy home*. You deserve it! Sometimes the positive aspects of a one-night stand can outweigh the potential damage to the psychic energy. You will leap up tomorrow morning feeling refreshed — a new man! Now run along — don't mind me! *Sex is natural!/Sex is good!/Not everybody does it —*"

"*—But everybody should!*" I chime. Amazing to think those lines were written by a heterosexual!

I go and talk to the guy. He's sort of quite nice. After some sophisticated verbal sparring we leave the Royal Oak and start walking back to my house. He explains that he is a go-ahead young designer from Richmond. He used to be from round here, he says, when he was a teenager.

"Lord, how it takes me back!" he sighs nostalgically. "It's a sentimental journey, and no mistake!" As we turn into my street he lowers his voice and says conspiratorially, "Shall I tell you a secret?"

"Go on," I reply.

"Well... I lost my virginity in a house in this street!... Happy memories!"

I can think of no reply, apart from "So did I," which somehow just doesn't seem very sophisticated. We walk on. As we get to the house and I start up the steps, I notice that he has lagged behind. I turn. He is standing looking up at the house with an astonished expression on his face. "You live in *this house*?" he gasps.

"Sure," I reply. "Why?"

He blinks. "This was the house!" he rasps.

"Which house?"

"The one where I lost my virginity!"

"No!"

"I swear to God!"

"Impossible," I tell him. Then I pause. Might as well check the story out! "When did this occur?" I probe.

He calculates. "Um... say... four years ago."

I reflect that it is possible, but... "Weird!" I mutter. As we go in, I work out how long I have been living in the house. It comes out as three years. Three and a half. I wonder how long Eric and Tookie had been in the house before I came. "What was the guy's name?" I enquire.

"Well, it was a sort of one-night stand sort of thing really," he confesses. "In fact, more of a sort of fifteen-minute stand. Wham, bam, thank you, Sam!" We both laugh. I begin to grow suspicious. "I'll be fucked if I can remember what he was called. He was really great-looking though. He had really short hair with a little quiff..."

"Sort of six foot-ish?" I venture.

"About that," says he. "So you know him!"

"My flatmate's boyfriend," I explain. "Small world!"

As we walk down the hall, he lingers by the stuffed fox head (sorry, but it wasn't my idea) that hangs opposite the door to the kitchen. "Yes! *Yes*! the *fox head*!" he mutters, as if miles away.

We go into the kitchen for a coffee. He looks round the room, an expression of shock mingled with joy playing about his features. "Yes . . . yes, I remember it well . . ." he rasps hoarsely. "The . . . table . . ."

The way he looks at the table and the somewhat obsessive way he caresses its surface confirms my worst fears. I quickly make the coffee and take him to my room, feeling that any memories he might harbour of a lusty work-out with Corey are bound to put me somewhat in the shade. I put on a record and we drink our coffee.

"Shall we perform sex now?" he asks.

We perform sex. When we have finished I considerately ask him how it was for him.

"Not bad," he replies, his mind evidently elsewhere. "But I must say it was nothing like as good as when your flatmate's boyfriend gave me a bloody good shafting over the kitchen table."

ELEVEN

"I forgot to think about the problem of the pesky Swede before and after," I confess.

"Before and after what?" says Eric.

We are on our way to Brighton. Me, Eric, Tookie and Barbara Honigsbaum. Thank goodness we managed to persuade Tookie to drive us down! And then at the last minute there was this sort of crisis with Barbara which I'll tell you more about later, and Tookie felt she really had to invite her along too, so suddenly there were four of us — quite a party!

I am a *leetle* bit concerned that we might prove a bit of an invasion when we all turn up at Roly's place, what with the baby and Christine not being very well, but Eric says not to worry. Apparently Roly's place is just gi-normous, and anyway, Roly used to be a boyfriend of Eric's and so Eric can do more or less what he wants. That's the theory, anyhow. Eric and Roly were a first-time teenage love affair — terrifically romantic! Both of them only seventeen! Roly's gorgeous and I must say it's lovely to think of the two of them in bed together, barely able to read but doing nicely without the help of manuals as they boldly explore love's strange new world! . . . How my mind wanders sometimes! Legend has it that Roly eventually got rather depressed by the whole business of being ostracized by the heterosexual patriarchy and decided that if he couldn't beat 'em he was going to join 'em. The whole difficult business of changing sexuality was managed in one effortless bound when he was fortunate enough to meet Christine, a girl who looks exactly like a boy, and he has been laughing ever since. One can't help being tempted to follow suit sometimes (he made it all look so easy) but two objections spring quickly to mind:

1) How many girls are there out there who look exactly like boys? (NB: I have always found it hard enough to find a boy FULL STOP, let alone one who is really a girl!)

and

2) — well, point number 2 is a bit of a delicate point actually. I don't even know if I should say it at all. It's just that I can't help wondering... no, my lips are sealed. Let me just say that I'm not entirely convinced that *this particular solution would work for me*. (I have always been a model of tact, and I don't intend to change now.)

"Before and after having sex," I tell him. "Really, Eric, your short-term memory seems to be somewhat in disrepair. You specifically told me that the best way of looking at a problem was before and then after having sex with a handsome man or willowy girlie. My point was that I didn't have a boyfriend so I'd have to go with a hand shandy. And then last night I did have sex, but I completely forgot all about what you said. So all in all it was a terrible waste of a rare opportunity."

"We'll find you a husband, don't you worry," laughs Tookie, hair resplendently orange today and heavy with plastic fruit and stuff.

"Don't you worry," echoes Barbara. I sit back and experience a warm glow as I reflect what marvellous friends I have, all pulling together as a team to try to haul me out of the ditch. Because it is a ditch, not having a boyfriend. You might as well be lying in a damp deep ditch by the side of the road for all the fun you have. Sometimes I think, This is just stupid, it's my fault, my standards are just too high. The obvious solution is not to be so picky. Just *go out and get myself a boyfriend*. I tell myself that there are just loads of guys out there who could turn out to be real fab — it's just a matter of giving them a chance. Give 'em a *chance*! I say to myself. *Don't be such a prude! Take 'em home, try 'em out, think it over*! So then I go down the Royal Oak and pick up some arsehole who tells me straight out that it wasn't as good as when — but let that rest. If that's what he felt, then that's what he felt, and the truth can't hurt you. But sometimes, when life ain't easy and love gets hard, I must confess I find this whole evolution process rather a strain, and before I know what I am thinking, I am energetically cursing the lovely Corey for no greater sin than just *being lovely*! That's how bitter and twisted it can make you, being single. Sometimes I look at some crabby woman in a shop and think, *Bet she hasn't had sex in a month*! — and then I am sobered by the ghastly consideration that I haven't had it in six — so what sort of crabby face am *I* going round wearing? Ah, life — life! What a strange, mad muddle you are!

You're probably dying to know what happened to Barbara. I must say she is an unending source of fascination. Well apparently she had what they call *artistic differences* with the director of the play which had been written specially for her, and so she said to the author, Either he goes or I go! Can you believe that? I must say we were all terribly impressed, you know, by her spunkiness in laying it on the line like this. Unfortunately, the upshot of it was that the director *stayed*, and that left Barbara with only one option. So she's coming down to Brighton with us to let off steam and get away from the whole wearing business of making oneself famous. Personally I am a tiny smidgeon concerned about Barbara's career, as, from what we can glean, her progress towards inevitable stardom seems to be regularly punctuated with incidents like this. It's not that I think her evidently very volatile artistic temperament might actually *prevent* her from becoming a star (far from it, it's very much a part of her unique talent) but I feel that perhaps it may unnecessarily prolong her apprenticeship — her time on the fringe of fame, as it were. But of course I keep very quiet about my opinions. Tookie would never forgive me if she discovered I had an opinion on Barbara Honigsbaum (other than how totally fab she is, of course).

So it looks like we're in for a real fun time as we tear down the motorway in Tookie's minibus (falling to bits!) towards the San Francisco of the British South Coast. It's kind of fun to think that the entire staff and clientele of the Stars of the Future Talent

Agency is on holiday together (Tookie only has two clients, Barbara and Eric — quality not quantity!) and all in all we can be sure that a fair amount of brainstorming will get done on the subject of both of their careers. Recently I have been worried that Tookie has been favouring Barbara over Eric in terms of hustling Hollywood producers and stuff — I mean, Eric really has been *at rest* for too long — but I feel sure that our Brighton jaunt is going to put everything straight, and that soon Eric will be leaping about the set of some megabucks-smasheroo alongside Harrison Ford and a cast of thousands. Positive thinking!

We get to Brighton at about seven. Big welcome from Roly and Christine — obviously surprised to see Tookie and Barbara but also delighted. I figure it will take them about ten minutes to twig that the girls want to stay too, so that means we have to start charming them without a second's delay. Bad news on one front, though: the place is *really small*. There *is* a spare room, which is going to be for the baby when it's a little older, but it's only got a single bed in it. Thank heavens we brought loads of sleeping bags!

We play with the baby (no one can quite believe Roly has managed to reproduce, but there's the evidence, as real as real can be!) and quiz our hosts about the pros and cons of living in Brighton. Not only is Christine absolutely knackered from not getting any sleep because of the baby, but also poor Roly is suffering from some mysterious complaint to do with his intestines. The doctors don't really know what it is and we're all very concerned. Eric and I urge him to go and see our marvellous homoeopath, but he shakes his head wearily and tells us that he thinks it has got "a bit beyond that stage". What he means by this I cannot imagine, and am about to harangue him for not believing in holistic medicine when I remember that it is absolutely vital to be incredibly polite for at least the next ten minutes. I bite back my tirade and save it for later.

As there is not much money floating about we have planned our stay with as much care as if it were the battle of Waterloo. We have three nights, and have decided on one treat per night. Tonight will be a slap-up but really very reasonable pizza dinner at the Duomo restaurant (where what you want is *not on the menu*, as they say); tomorrow night will be the movies (silly in a way to go to the movies when you're in a fab seaside town, but on the other hand it is undeniably true that the salt air does make you feel trashy, and I know from long experience that there is absolutely no point in trying to fight it); and Saturday night will be a strictly only-window-shopping visit to the rather buzzy little disco in the basement of the what's-it's-name hotel, just down the sea-front from the pier. These are the three treats; there will of course be quite a lot of ambling through the romantic little streets, window-shopping in both senses, and, providing we are sensible and drink halves, a healthy amount of pub-crawling. We also have a lump of extremely strong Lebanese, which frankly must have opium or something in it because it sends me completely out of my box at the merest puff, and *that's* not a thing you can say about most of the stuff you buy these days. This will be smoked back at Roly's tonight and tomorrow night after the pubs close. You probably think we're mad to have worked everything out so precisely, but I can tell you, when you're in a party of four (or six, if Roly and Christine can forget the baby for a while and come aboard the Good Ship Party) it really pays to have a game-plan. Of course, we are keeping our mouths shut about our ideas for the weekend because officially we're only staying one night, but our plan is to take Roly and Chris out to dinner at the Duomo and get them drunk and then take them home and get them really stoned, and sort of get them to the point when they can't really *not* offer, quite spontaneously, to extend the invitation. There is a point, I think, when you're drunk — certainly when you're stoned — when the party-principle sort of takes over, and it is actually quite difficult not to go for it. So anyway, it is absolutely vital that we get them to come along to the dinner, and we start working on them almost immediately.

Problems at the first hurdle: if there's one thing Roly *can't* do, it's go out to dinner. His insides are just too fucked. Apparently he's on a diet of dry bread and water or something. Christine, for some reason, doesn't want to come either. She says she hasn't got a babysitter, which seems absurd seeing as Roly's going to be home, but she is quite Adam Ant about the whole thing and in the end we go without them.

As we have a gander at the menu we try to work out an alternative plan. Roly and Chris probably won't be able to say no to all four of us staying tonight, but unless we can do some serious charming the thing might well have turned sour by Friday sundown, and we certainly don't want to start incurring hotel bills.

"Well," muses Eric, "we can always get Lenny off our hands if he is prepared to use the Slag Method."

I am outraged. "I never use the Slag Method, as you very well know," I snap, glancing round the restaurant to see if my favourite waiter is working tonight (I'm sure sure SURE he's a same-sexer, but these Mediterraneans do have such a terrible time coming to terms with their orientation. They never get beyond Identity Denial most of the time. I had an Italian boyfriend once who had got hopelessly bogged down in a particularly nasty case of Identity Tolerance, and I must say he drove me mad. Apparently some Mediterranean men have sex with other guys quite a lot, but *only if the other guy is in drag!* Can you believe that? And these guys — the ones not in drag — are convinced that they're not really same-sexers, just normal hetero patriarchs on for a jokey sort of laugh or two, and they go back to their wives, *etc., etc., etc.,* and what's more are *absolutely horrid* to same-sexers who are a bit more up-front about it all, and beat them up and things. But I digress). "Use the slag method yourself," I pout. "Everyone's always so fucking hot for your arse. You could wear the cycle-shorts."

Benevolent smile. "My God, Lenny, you do need a boyfriend, don't you? Snapping about like some sort of piranha . . ."

My indignation rises. "No, actually, Eric," (cross, straight-faced) "actually I think it's quite a good idea. Roly's place is obviously too small for all seven of us, and I think it would be a real help if we could somehow lessen the load. You're much more attractive than me and could pull it off with your eyes closed. Out you go! I'm sure a lot of men in Brighton would be only too pleased to accommodate you for the weekend."

"Oh, put a sock in it and read the menu," says he, quite unruffled.

I count to ten. Then I resume, much calmed and very nearly serene, "It's not fair for you to make me focus on my emotional problems. It's extremely bad for my chakras."

"OK, I didn't mean it, it was a joke, OK?" says he.

I am satisfied. I read the menu. The air is thick with fragrances of sage . . . garlic . . . tomato paste . . .

We have a delicious meal and the evening is a great success.

We get back at about 11.30 and Roly and Chris have *gone to bed*! Can you believe that? But we have a key, so we let ourselves in. On the kitchen table is a very sweet note which says:

Hi guys! – 'Fraid we're knackered and we've decided to get some shut-eye before the baby's next feeding time. Tell the girls that if they want to stay they can crash out in the sitting room, but I hope they brought sleeping bags cos we really weren't expecting them. Sleep well,
Roly and Chris. XX.

We're heart-broken that Roly and Chris have gone to bed (no opportunity to get them stoned and wear down their resistance) but we decide to look on the bright side. It is fairly apparent that our only course of action is to get absolutely hog-snarling on the Leb, which we get on with without further ado. Tookie finds an old yoghurt-pot in Roly and Chris's kitchen dustbin and improvises a very successful hubble-bubble. We smoke the Leb through lime juice. I am already scared by this point, because as I'm sure you know, a hubble-bubble is the way to get stoned stoned STONED. The smoke is cooled down so it doesn't hurt your throat, so you just gulp down loads, and before you know where you are, YOU TOO are picking up transmissions from the planet Fargon! Anyway, the idea is you *drink the juice afterwards* and this stuff *really* does the business. We steal a tiny smidgeon-widgeon-*pigeon* of vodka from Roly and Chris's drinks cabinet and whop in a couple of icecubes and KAPOW!! Your attention please! We leave for the moon in 'zackly *three minutes*! Later Eric gets the Tarot cards out (always fatal) and things actually start getting a bit heavy. At one point Tookie throws a *small* saucepan up towards the ceiling and *it doesn't come down again*. Never. The saucepan does not come down. We look up and it's not stuck to the ceiling. We look down and it's not on the floor. It has completely disappeared. It just went up and didn't come down. After this we all feel distinctly freaked-out so we go to bed.

TWELVE

They say that rock 'n roll is the Devil's music, and my studies have confirmed this to be the case. Certainly it played a crucial role on the day on which I lost that which can never be regained.

Now, one of the fundamental rules of soul-catching as Barney and I had been taught it by our over-lively church was that you always always ALWAYS do it in pairs. I think the idea was that in this way you would be more able to cope if you rang someone's doorbell and the door was *actually opened by Lucifer himself*. Barney and I were not, on the whole, rule-breakers, and we never seriously questioned the wisdom of this principle. But on one particular evening a temptation to err too strong to resist was placed in our way by the Foul Fiend, and err we did. We had tickets to see Pink Floyd, you see, and we were rather behind in our soul-catching. A road could take anything up to two hours to service, depending on how garrulous the inhabitants might be, and our strict superiors at the church had set us a quota to get through by Sunday *or else*. We didn't enquire *or else what?* We were, however, sufficiently terrified to want to get our quota finished, while also quite appalled by the prospect of being late for the opening of the gig, which, rumour had it, made your mind explode into a zillion brightly-coloured splinters. To cut a long story short, Barney and I split up for the last street we had to do. I took the odd numbers and he took the even ones. The street was the street in which I now reside. Number 13 — unlucky for some, no doubt — proved to be for me a door to another world.

As it turned out, Barney and I were not late for the ineffable opening of the Pink Floyd gig. Only, it was not strictly speaking the Lenny he knew and, in his own boring way, loved, who accompanied him that night. It was a fiend in humanoid form. *I had changed!*

And indeed, how I *have* changed! Changed, changed, changed! To think that I once sweated blood over the application form for the job at the Hammersmith Wholefood Emporium, and all over one silly little question: *Are you gay or straight?* Looking back on it now, I must say I feel it was perhaps a teensy bit rude of them to ask such a question in the first place, though I'm sure they meant well. One would expect people whose diet consisted of a high percentage of raw and organic produce to have a more instinctive understanding of the whole matter of orientation, vexed though it undoubtedly is. There is no such thing as gay, of course, and there is no such thing as straight (the fact that my mouth waters whenever I see a picture of Aidan Quinn is quite beside the point). All there is is people. When, oh when will this tired old world finally see this simple truth? — a truth that has been staring it in the face for the past twenty zillion years. How long, O Lord, how long . . . ?

Now as I sit in Roly and Chris's very restful sitting room (decorated entirely in white — pesky Swede please take note), calmly filling in my application form for the post of Second Assistant Editor at the Shafter Press, I cannot help pausing awhile, the toxic tip of my pencil melting soothingly on my tongue, and reflecting upon how things change, and we with them! How buds blossom, how ripened things rot! I have written in answers to all their questions about my previous employers and my qualifications, and I have come to what is obviously intended as the prickly one, the one that is going to separate the sheep from the goats. It goes like this:

How comfortable, in your opinion, would you feel about coming into daily contact with visual material of an explicitly sexual nature?
1) Extremely uncomfortable
2) Slightly uncomfortable
3) Neither comfortable nor uncomfortable
4) Moderately comfortable
5) Completely comfortable

Why, extremely comfortable, of course! I circle the 5) carefully. I am pleased to say that I have worked my way up through the six stages of enlightenment and arrived, relatively unscathed, at the happy state of Identity Integration. I would go so far as to say I have come through with flying colours! No hang-ups for Lenny Carnegie! (that's my surname, by the way: Carnegie). It is my firm belief that the humanoid body is beautiful, much though many embittered old puritans would have us believe otherwise, and so are its functions. Personally I don't feel the need for a library groaning with photographic records of other people's unclothed appearances, or their various ascents of the many steep cliff-faces of satisfaction, but I would defend to the death the right of my fellow man to retire to such a place, if that was where he felt he wanted to spend any portion of his allotted sublunary time. The only problems I can see about the magical world of porno are the subtle karmic implications of handing over cash for a gawp at a guy's willy — but hey! this is something that each one of us has to sort out with his own immortal and extraterrestrial soul.

Anyway, here I sit filling in my application form while Eric and Tookie and Barbara Honigsbaum get some serious brainstorming done on the subject of their careers. We all slept like logs, incidentally — I love sleeping on the floor. Barbara has a bad back and so we let her have the one bed and Eric was too big for the sofa so Tookie had that. I must say I was the first up, and that was at midday! You can't beat a good holiday, can you? I rather wickedly rolled a joint and we all smoked it over breakfast (promising promising promising to ourselves to go and re-stock Roly and Christine's fridge just as soon as the effect of the caffeine takes hold). Roly's at work now, and Chris has taken the baby out for some reason — they've gone to the doctor or the baby-minder or something — don't ask me what it was, I'm hopeless with kids! If it isn't one thing it's another!

A lot of merry laughter from the other side of the room, where the brainstorming is going on. "OK, then," I tell them, "spill the beanz, and it had better be good because you're making it quite impossible for me to do my application form." Well, apparently Eric and Barbara have come up with a real winner this time. Eric sort of wanted to do a revival of the thing about the three cowboys where he played the dead body, but Barbara wasn't really on for it because she couldn't really see a role for herself (well, there *are* some female roles but they don't really get a look-in on the crucifixion scene, which is the best bit). Then Eric made a sudden quantum leap and realized that they absolutely must must MUST do a science-fiction version of Noel Coward's enduring and much-loved old stoater, *Private Lives*. Eric could have a green face and pointy ears and Barbara could wear *any number* of wild outfits made of coat-hangers and silver foil, like Zsa Zsa Gabor in *Queen of Outer Space*. A sort of hush descends upon the room, and we all feel that we are in the presence of something greater than any of us. It's a bit like when the saucepan disappeared. No one knows exactly where the idea came from, it just seemed to fall out of the sky. It is so completely apparent to all of us that this idea absolutely *cannot fail* to make Eric and Barbara into stars, that for a while none of us even feels the need to say so. We just sit, dazed and confused, even a little frightened at the thought of the fame which we are all soon going to have to learn how to handle. They say it hits hard at first, fame, but after a bit you grow to like it. The clever ones rise above it, of course, concentrate their minds on an ecstatic vision of samadhi or whatever it's called and carry on as before. But the others — the ones with fewer spiritual resources — they get dependent on it and it turns into a *drug*. I actually know what I'm talking about here, though you probably think I'm just making it up. I once knew — no, I can't tell you. You wouldn't believe me. Let's just say I once knew someone who is now a VERY BIG STAR INDEED, and he won't even acknowledge my presence any more, let alone talk to me.

Tookie promises that she will clear the rights with the Noel Coward estate just as soon as we get back to town, and the calm and professional way she says it sends shivers down all our spines. A great tidal wave of vibe-energy floods over us like some tremendous flood. We leap up and rush out into the sunny Brighton streets. The sky is clear and blue, the air salty and fresh. The houses look like somebody's dream. We bound down the street at a level of exactly two inches above the ground at all times. Tookie says she knows a fabulous director-designer team who have been doing some *very weird* stuff recently, and she just knows they'll go for it. I mean, science-fiction Noel Coward! — are we talking wild or are we talking *wild*? I ask if I can play one of the minor parts and everyone sighs tolerantly and explains that you have to have an Equity card to act. I'll get one! I say. Easier said than done, they reply. Apparently you have to be hired as an actor to get a card, and in order to get hired as an actor *you have to have a card*. "Then how did *you* get one, Eric?" I snap, feeling that this is all rather unfair, and that they probably just don't want to share their fame with me because I'm short and look like a lamb. (Actually I'd probably be rather good in a science-fiction show, I mean I could play an alien, couldn't I? I wouldn't even need make-up!) Eric laughs and says he got his Equity card by being a stripper. Oh yes, Eric, very funny, I reply. No, it's true, says he, that's the big loophole: cabaret work. If you want to get a card by acting you have to put in a hundred days' work or something, but if you're prepared to waggle your schlong on a tawdry wooden stage in front of a hundred sex-starved piss-heads you only need to put in twelve. It's a sort of joke on the part of the organizers of Equity, rather like the pranks that older boys play on younger boys at boarding schools. Drudgery or Humiliation. Well, that's as may be, I reply, but Eric, please don't expect me to believe that you disrobed on stage. I may be gullible, but I am not stark staring bonkers. Believe what you want, says he. What a wind-up merchant!

The streets seem to be choc-a-bloc with handsome same-sexers and, as so often is the case, the ghastly spectre of overstimulation rears its ugly head. I divert the party into a trendy bookshop where I hope to find a quiet space in which to draw breath, and quite by chance we find Dave's book of short stories on the shelf! We have great fun explaining to Barbara that Dave is our intimate friend (more famous than you, girlie!) and urge her to invest in a copy. The old snoot is apparently too good for Dave's marvellous book, and in the end Eric and I have to team up and buy a copy and give it to the old cart-horse as a present. She thanks us very sweetly, with a big routine about how much she's going to love reading it (her first gay book! — my, Barbara, but you're liberal these days!) but you can't fool Lenny Carnegie. I have a fair idea that Miss High Class is just a tiny smidgeon jealous of our famous pal and his exciting and successful stories.

The day flies by, and we finish it off with a movie, as planned. Gripping thriller. Great scene at the end where the sort-of hero has to run away to New York but he hasn't got any money, so he hangs around in the airport car-park giving blow-jobs until he's saved up the price of the air-fare. On the way home we have one of those rather pointless *What-would-you-have-done?* conversations, which is really just everyone's way of being too embarrassed to admit the shameful fact that it was a real turn-on to think of this cute guy servicing all those greasy businessmen. It shouldn't have been a turn-on, but it was. Lots of things that shouldn't be turn-ons are. The humanoid soul, alas, has a dark side that longs for ecstatic bondage just as its sunnier side yearns to soar. No doubt those of us who are outraged by the facts of this corporeal life will be provided with an opportunity to have it out with their Maker at some duly appointed time after they have taken leave of it.

We get back to find none other than the lovely Corey ensconced in the sitting room with a joint in one hand and a vodka-and-lime in the other. Apparently the Heath has been really quiet, like a funeral in fact, so he has decided to join us in Brighton.

"Roly and Chris have gone to bed," he adds.

THIRTEEN

Another glorious day! Must say I slept like a log yet again, even though we were packed onto the sitting-room floor like sardines. We get up and find a note from Roly and Chris. Apparently they completely forgot, but they had arranged to go away to stay with Chris's mum and dad in Littlehampton for the weekend and show them the baby etc., etc., etc. They've already gone. We are all heartbroken, of course, that we won't be seeing them, but on the other hand it does mean that there'll be more room in the flat.

We go to make breakfast and realize with horror that we completely forgot to restock the fridge, and for a moment things look black indeed. We have drunk all the orange juice and milk, and eaten all the bacon and eggs and cheese and stuff. We've even eaten all the bread. The ghastly spectre of the *trip to the shops on an empty stomach* rears its abominable head. Then we notice that there's a deep freeze. Big sigh of relief. We get out some bread and whop it in the micro, and then spend a happy time rummaging through a wide selection of absolutely mouth-watering breakfast possibilities (promising promising promising, in fact *tying knots in our handkerchieves* to the effect that we will do a major shop before we go back) and finally get some major munchies going. Yes, you guessed it, we're on the wicked weed again, even though it's only two o'clock in the afternoon. You probably think we're completely wild and out of order but I'm afraid we're on holiday and that's all there is to it. You probably take lots of drugs yourself, caffeine and nicotine and stuff, so just get off our backs, OK?

After brunch we realize that if we don't get out of the house soon the best of the day will be past, so we decide to ration ourselves to just one last spliff, which we enjoy with some very strong coffee from Roly and Chris's espresso machine. When the effect of the caffeine takes hold we spring to our feet and leap out into the street. We are amazed to find that it is already dark! It seems impossible that we have spent all day having breakfast. For a while Tookie tries to cling to the idea that maybe we went through a time-warp when the effects of the last spliff took hold, but unfortunately we are not *quite* stoned enough to let her get away with that one, and are therefore forced to face up to the fact that we have been rather lazy — but hey! it's these lazy days that one remembers in years to come, isn't it? — days on which one did absolutely fuck-all, but for a brief magical moment *everything seemed to make sense*.

We get to the pier and *my God* it all looks colourful in our present state. We go on the chairaplanes and Barbara is sick. The good thing about being stoned is you don't have to go through the motions of commiserating with people when they've been sick if you don't want to, you don't have to pretend to be all concerned, you can just ignore them and you have the brilliant excuse that you're too stoned to care. The pier, of course, has its quota of same-sexers, and soon my mind is straying back to that old chestnut, the contents of a man's trousers. Needless to say, going round in a group which includes the ravishing Corey has a drawback the size of the Ritz to it, namely that all eyes are drawn to his superior beauty, leaving the plain and the lamb-like shivering in an icy oblivion of forgottenness. But far be it from me to bleat. There is a very good bit in *Blinded by the Light* which says that everyone gets a handsome man or willowy girlie in the end. It's just a matter of faith. And you can hang around in bars as much as you like, and you can answer lonely hearts ads and all the rest of it, but the fact of the matter is there's a Grand Scheme of things and it's all been fixed in this special department in heaven, and when your handsome man or willowy girlie comes along, you'll know all about it. You might be just sauntering down Hammersmith Grove, or pausing in the Wholefood Emporium, lingering between the mung beans and the yeast flakes. You might be at the straightest party you ever were at, at Auntie Irene and Uncle George's perhaps – in fact Auntie Irene *might even introduce him to you!* You see, you really can't predict these things, and so all you can do is just have faith.

After the pier we gracefully steer the evening towards the concept of a dignified crawl round the prime same-sexer pubs, trying not to make it too obvious to the delicate Barbara that this is in fact the plan. Luckily she is too stoned to notice. Actually I believe that life is in some ways very simple for Barbara Honigsbaum, in that her faith in her power to mesmerize all members of the male sex with her astonishing beauty is absolute, and it will take more than a night of being ignored by same-sexers to shake it. Tonight, at any rate, her resistance is low and we manage to get to the marvellous disco in the hotel basement without so much as a whimper of protest from her corner. Once inside I make straight for the bar, looking neither to right nor to left, determined to get through at least the first five minutes without being overwhelmed in a torrent of stimulus. I fix my mind on a vision of a soothing rum-and-coke and tell myself that the contents of a man's trousers are of no more interest to me than the contents of the Dead Sea Scrolls. But of course it doesn't work. All around me are hot, sweet-smelling male bodies, vibrant with youth and vitality, stripped down to vests and tight T's – dressed up – dressed down. Leather jackets, big packets, into it, into it! And then I am clutching the cold sides of the wash-basin and feverishly dousing myself down and trying to say my alphabet backwards. I get through the whole backwards alphabet but it hasn't worked. I try to think about Income Tax and funerals and carbon monoxide and Margaret Thatcher but my internal tempest continues to rage. I decide that I should have pressed on to the bar rather than fleeing into the gents for the old de-stimulation routine, and that the rum-and-coke was probably exactly what I needed. I remind myself that I am very, very stoned, and things are probably not as serious as they seem.

Soon we are all drinking and joking and strutting our stuff and the evening is a great success. Corey makes a "new friend". A "new friend" is the term employed in our very evolved circles for someone with whom Corey intends to have carnal relations. It is fairly apparent that this "new friend" (seventeen, spotty, gormless, doe-eyed, great bum) is giving His Loveliness the serious hots, because if that were not the case I am pretty sure the old shafter wouldn't be subjecting himself and us to what is — call us all old-fashioned — an extremely embarrassing set-up. I mean, Corey could (to be absolutely brutal about it) just take the boy out the back of the place and enjoy him unceremoniously among the dustbins and beercrates, couldn't he? and that would be the end of it — not that I personally would risk my karmic balance in such a fashion, but Corey could, and still remain quite blissfully serene. And then it would be out of the way and we could all carry on as before. But no, it seems that Eric's boyfriend has other plans. You must remember, of course, that by the terms of their "Manifesto" Corey can only enjoy his "new friends" *once*, otherwise the whole deal with Eric would be off. Now, Corey is spinning us all some rather complicated story about how this boy is actually *from London* and he's only in Brighton for the day, and his date (some ageing lecher to whom he became unfortunately attached via a naive dabbling in the lonely hearts columns) has ditched him alone and friendless on the South Coast, and obviously we must take the boy under our wing and at least make sure he has a roof over his head for the night, and hey! there'll be room for one more in the minibus when we go back, won't there? We all say yes, of course, poor boy! etc., etc., etc., and before we know where we are our party has swelled to six. As we walk back to Roly and Chris's pad I ponder the arcane significances of these matters. I decide that Corey is definitely planning his enjoyment of his "new friend" with minute precision, and that, far from settling for less-than-ideal conditions, he has decided to go for nothing less than the full five-star three-lemons-in-a-row option, namely the one involving the use of our venerable old kitchen table for practices not strictly culinary. I don't let on to Eric, of course, that this is the way my cogitations are leading me, as I am not completely clear on the subtle point of, well, *exactly how open their relationship actually is*. I mean, is

Corey protecting the less evolved Eric from full knowledge of the hard realities? We all know, of course, that humankind cannot bear very much reality. At least, that's what someone once said, and my studies have repeatedly proved it to be the case. *Just how much does Eric know?* I often come back to this old teaser, and I must say, as the years have gone by it hasn't shown signs of being any more ready to render up its answer.

Getting hog-whimpering stoned is a great smoother-out of ruffles on the social lake, and this is the course of action we very sensibly plump for when we get back to the flat. Eventually it is bedtime. Funny vibe. Embarrassment. Gormless boy obviously hot for contents of Corey's 501s. Obviously not fully clued-up on state-of-play. Corey takes boy into kitchen (some hollow mention of coffee). Fills in (one assumes) gaps in boy's knowledge — or at least, strings him along with some complicated bullshit which it would be foolish even to guess at. Long and short of it: boy put on ice. Eric and Corey get Roly and Chris's double. Barbara in the single, Tookie on the sofa. I insist on the floor (rather like it) and boy is given no choice: floor or nothing, matey. Seems perfectly happy.

I drift off into an uneasy, twice-drugged sleep and am tormented by dreams involving a thousand different manifestations of Bibi, each one lovelier than the last. I am arrested in Morocco on some trumped-up charge. I am thrown into jail without trial, squealing of my innocence to no effect. The prison warder is none other than the Man For Whom I Yearn, resplendent in a blue-black uniform, tight round the arse, with S&M cap, mirror shades, truncheon and cuffs. "Strip!" he barks. I tremulously obey. "Now get those hands up against the wall and spread your legs!" My mind reels. What devilish contravention of the Geneva Convention is this? "I demand to speak to my lawyer!" I squeak. "I said spread 'em!" he snarls, poking my skinny butt with the tip of his truncheon, "Wider! . . . wider! . . ." I obey. Well, what choice do I have? If I cried out, who would hear? "I declare that if I spread them any wider I shall simply fall over," I point out. For answer comes nothing but a sharp, cynical laugh. My indignation rises as I feel the probing tip of Bibi's truncheon explore my nether anatomy, impertinently prising my buttocks apart as if seeking to enter and impale me and . . . black gloved hands roughly grasp at my... I wriggle and writhe on my rucked sheets, feebly trying to wake up, crying out to the heavens and all the spirits and vibes that rule our destinies to deliver me from the intolerable fires of unconsummated lust!

I wake up. I sit up. I want to piss. I go to the bathroom. In the mirror I see a ridiculous lamb-face, haggard from over-indulgence and sexual frustration. I think of Bibi's transcendent beauty that shames the desert sunset, and impotently curse my fate.

O what must I do to be free?

FOURTEEN

I have already apologized for the stuffed fox head which hangs in our hallway opposite the door that leads to the kitchen, and I will do so again. I don't approve, and I'm embarrassed to be associated with it. The fact that the poor creature was already dead was no excuse for Eric's buying the hideous trophy second-hand in Brick Lane and then sticking it up in our bloody hall. It seems to me as obvious as the day is long that animals have as much right to a decent burial as the rest of us, and the hanging of fox heads on the walls of human habitations is surely little more than the victorious crowings of the blood-sated beast, twentieth century or no twentieth century. One day I shall just take it down and whop it in the dustbin, and I just won't care when the rest of my oh-so-ideologically-groovy household gives me a hard time about it. Sometimes you've just got to stick up for your principles, popular or otherwise.

The fox head, however, plays a part in my tale. My tale of how I lost that which can never be regained, I mean. It's funny how you remember little things — little insignificant things like a joke made over tea, or the colour of someone's jacket — details that didn't mean much at the time, and still don't mean much when they come bounding back into your mind's eye years later, all fresh and glowing with a sense of their own importance, like puppies. And the really important things — like the face of the first boy you ever fell in love with, for example — refuse to come back to you, no matter how loud you call. Take the fox head, for example. It's ridiculous, I know, but whenever I see that fox head I can't help remembering how funny it looked when Corey hung my underpants on it. Because that was what he did. After he had successfully removed them from me, he turned, aimed carefully, and flung my C&A Y-fronts across the room and out into the hall to land gracefully on the severed head of the fox, where they remained like a tea-towel over a parrot's cage until I had served my purpose and was dismissed. Little meaningless memories!

Sometimes, when mellow, I look back to that day upon which I received the brief but glorious accolade of being permitted to play port to Corey's storm-tossed ship (for passion is a storm — lest we forget!) and I am unable not to feel a tiny glow of pride. That such a worm-like, insignificant apology for a man as I should have been so privileged! To have been allowed a seat in the very front of the stalls — nay, to have been up there *on stage* with The Man After Whom All Men Yearn, to have witnessed at the closest of close quarters a true master of his art, at the height of his powers, in the act of creation — surely, if only for this, I will be able to depart this life when my time comes without feeling that my existence has been entirely devoid of meaning. I tell myself that there must be men all over London who would give their right arms for a ticket to such a show — that I am in possession of sacred, almost arcane knowledge, comparable to that which binds Freemasons together in secret brotherhood; that I have gazed upon, nay *possessed*, what is in some ways the Holy Grail of London's alternative same-sexer scene. And these thoughts are a great comfort to me. Sometimes I even idly wonder what my special knowledge of Corey's intimate shafting habits might be worth on the open market. What would they all give, I wonder, to know whether or not he keeps his boots on? (he did); how many times he unburdens himself of his manly essences? (once, in my case); if he has any *funny little quirks*? In answer to that last burning question I think the answer has to be a resounding Yes, because, having carefully gone over my conversation with the guy I picked up in the Royal Oak that night, and remembering the way he looked at the fox head before we went into the kitchen, I think we may confidently suppose that the whole flinging of the underwear onto the fox is something of a ritual with the Master, something quite indispensable to his full, five-star, three-lemons-in-a-row enjoyment of the fleshly male. I think we may even postulate that *the linking of the underpants with the fox head gives us a vital clue as to Corey's true hidden nature as a trophy-hunter.* But Lord! how I rave!

When Corey opened the door ("Hello we're from the local church and were just wondering whether you were interested in Father God or Christ Jesus at all and whether you might like to invite them into your life at all and if not whether you might like to talk about it at all and if not *why not* and if not not NOT then is there anyone else in the house who you think *might* be interested in Father God or Christ Jesus . . . at all?") — when Corey opened the door, I thought I'd died and gone to heaven. And, judging by the look on his face, that is what Corey's latest "new friend" believes has happened to him, as we sit in this harshly-lit motorway service station mooning over coffee and doughnuts at three o'clock in the morning. I know he's probably half-asleep and not really with-it, but the boy is just staring at the — well, actually, I'm embarrassed to say it. Corey's leaning back on a chair, balancing on the two back legs, with his legs wide apart (as one does) and this boy (as one surely *doesn't*) is just staring at Corey's faded denim button-up fly as if a shaft of light is about to burst right out of it and transport him bodily to planet Fargon to the sound of a wild guitar solo. Personally I am so embarrassed I don't know where to look, but no one else seems to have noticed. Eric and I are on the next table. Oh yes, I forgot to tell you, the minibus has broken down.

"Perhaps there is a solution," says Eric, carefully spooning six spoonfuls of sugar into his tea.

I sigh wearily. "Eric, please don't start on your Zen-and-the-art-of-minibus-maintenance routine. We all know that your ignorance of the workings of the internal combustion engine approaches the poetic, so give it a rest, OK?"

"I didn't mean the minibus, I meant you."

"Oh." Why is it that I never seem to know what Eric is talking about?

"Perhaps there is a solution for *you*."

My tone becomes a tad frosty. "I wasn't aware that I was in need of a solution," I sniff.

"*You know*," says he, "*your boyfriend problem.*"

"If you're going to be patronizing about it I think I'd rather read the advice column in *Cosmo*," I snap.

Eric snorts with laughter. "If you don't get down to some good old touchy-feely within the next four weeks or so, I think you're going to sprout a second head or something," he murmurs with exasperating serenity.

"If I want to know your views I'll ask," I announce, and take a sip on my cold and watery coffee. Then, of course, I become curious. "I suppose it's absolutely earth shattering, this idea of yours . . ." I mutter.

"Actually, it is," says my flatmate jauntily (thank goodness he's so serene! I reflect — otherwise he would have stopped talking to me years ago.) "My plan is this: *we give a party!*"

I am dumbstruck. The simplicity of it — the beauty of it!

"We've got a fab house — plenty of space — we know loads of same-sexers — it's the festive season — what more do we need? Your dance-card will be full before you can say Jack Robinson!" he babbles.

"Yes — yes," I blurt; "we can wait until Bjorn has gone home for his Christmas holiday! It'll be fab!"

Eric pulls out a pad of paper and a pencil. Thank goodness he's had all those years of experience in the Community Health Council! I realize with a warm glow of satisfaction that he's going to take notes. He licks the toxic tip of the pencil, furrows his brow, and writes:

Party
1) Wait till pesky Swede away for Xmas.
"What else?"

"Um . . . *network*," I reply. "Write down *network*, or *networking* maybe . . ."

"How about: *network in Hammersmith and Shepherds Bush same-sexer community . . . ?*"

I am beside myself. "Yes! Yes! Write it down!" I cry.

Eric writes. For a second we are both lost in thought.

"Do we want it to be a challenging party or just a fun one?"

I muse.

"What's the difference?" he asks, rather obtusely.

I snort with disbelief. "A challenging party, as you very well know, is one with strippers and porno-vids and things, whereas a fun party—"

"Wait a minute," he interrupts, putting down his notepad and pencil; "*what have you been reading?*"

"I thought everyone knew that," I reply, amazed.

"Never heard such a load of rubbish in my entire life," says he. "You want sleazy? We make it sleazy. You want classy? We make it classy. It's your party. But don't start bombarding me with half-baked bullshit about 'challenging parties' just because you want to rub Baby Oil into Rick's pecs but haven't got the nerve to say."

"If you're going to be like this then I don't think I want a party at all," I pout. (Damn! damn! damn! What am I saying??)

"Suit yourself."

I bite my lip, and pray he'll forget I was crabby about the party idea. I know full well it is my only hope. He probably will.

The minibus is called *The Enterprise*, and it's a left-over from Tookie's days as manager of the Stars of the Future Theatre Company, which was, until this marvellously productive weekend of brainstorming, sadly defunct, but which we are all now confident will rise phoenix-like from its own ashes for the forthcoming groundbreaking production of *Private Lives 2000*, starring Eric and Barbara. Luckily *The Enterprise* has got AA insurance, and so all is not lost. Soon a man in shining armour is going to come and rescue us from the intolerable nightmare our journey home has become. A little note here: I think Tookie is a tiny nadger cross with Corey for charming her into taking his "new friend" back with us in the bus. She often jokes about how *The Enterprise* is about to "break up", in a special Scotty voice. "She canna take any more, Captain," she will chirp in her very passable Scotty imitation, "She'll break up!" Well, Tookie seemed to be of the opinion that *The Enterprise* shouldn't really be asked to carry more than five people at the outside, especially on such a long journey, and she *kept on saying* (in her fun voice, of course) that she was worried she might "break up". As it happens, that is exactly what has come to pass, and so, even though she was probably only joking about it before, she now feels, I think, just a little tiny nadger of real crossness about the whole thing, though crossness proper isn't really in her character. I think she feels that all of us sitting around in a motorway service station for hours and hours in the middle of the night is rather a disproportionately high price to pay for the pleasure of knowing that Corey is going to get his end away.

Eventually the AA man arrives and repairs the minibus. Huge sigh of relief. We are actually not far from home in terms of miles — somewhere in the wilds of South London — and we are all confident that we shall be safely tucked up in our beds in not much more than two shakes of a lamb's tail. We stock up on chocolate milk and coke and stuff and a sort of fun vibe returns to the proceedings. But just as we are about to leave the service station, Corey takes Tookie to one side and says something about his new friend absolutely having to crash *in his own home*, and how he knows it's a pain but he also knows Tookie will understand. Apparently the boy wears contact lenses and he's run out of fluid or something, and so he simply has to get home. At this point Tookie's unshakably cheerful expression becomes a little glazed. "Where does the boy live?" she enquires. "Uxbridge," says Corey, shifting from foot to foot and looking at the ground. Lucky for him he's such a complete charmer!

When the rest of us hear we're going home via Uxbridge the party vibe fades again. We get that terrible nightmarish feeling that we have in fact died and gone to hell, and this is what it's like, forever driving back from Brighton to London, forever breaking down, forever being diverted, never getting home. Conversation becomes sparse. After what seems like an eternity we get to Uxbridge and drop the boy outside his house. He thanks Tookie gormlessly for the lift, takes one last longing look at Corey's crotch and takes his leave. We turn round and set off for Hammersmith. Halfway along the Westway we run out of petrol. Tookie goes *very quiet*, and, though of course this is only a guess, I would say that she might even be regretting she ever offered to drive us to Brighton and back in the first place. Corey and Barbara are fast asleep by this time, and so Eric and I get out and set off into the cold night with a petrol can, hoping to find a garage.

"Corey is a one!" I chuckle.

"Isn't he dreadful?" smiles Eric, indulgent as ever.
"But then of course, that's half his charm," I point out.
"At least half," says Eric.

FIFTEEN

Next day I get up at three. Thank heavens I'm a waiter, not a milkman or something! At work there is a big buzz in the place because there's a costume-fitting session in progress. All the waiters are being measured up for their dresses, and are very excited about the whole thing. My heart sinks. I can't help feeling I've been tricked somewhere along the line. Certainly my contract of employment makes no mention of ladies' clothing. Worst of all is the consideration that my lovely Moroccan workmate (and friend!!) will see me looking even more ridiculous than usual. The only way I can manage not to run screaming for the door is by reminding myself that I do not wish to be financially embarrassed over Christmas, and fixing my mind on a beatific vision of Bibi in a G-string.

I am told that my dress is going to be quite sensational, with little fairy-lights woven into it so that I will actually light up like a Christmas tree. Light up like a Christmas tree indeed! This is what I hate about drag. What biological woman would ever want to light up like a Christmas tree? Exactly. Real women have more sense. What man would ever want to go out with a woman who lit up like a Christmas tree? I rest my case. Drag is surely the last refuge of the almost-sectionable, among whose number I do not yet count myself; nor will I, neither — not before I have gone at least another six months without finding myself a boyfriend. Actually I'm being a bit harsh here. Some of my best friends are drag-queens, and of course at its best it is a highly evolved art form.

I grind my teeth as I am strapped into a padded bra and measured by a leering tailor, whose hellish speciality (one assumes) this is. "Done any cabaret before?" he simpers, pins between teeth. My ears burn hotly with chagrin. I particularly resent the way the word "cabaret" seems to have been hijacked and forcibly yoked to the meaning of men swishing around in frocks doing lip-sync to tired old Liza Minelli numbers. "No," I mutter, glancing round the bar to check that Bibi can't see me. "No, I, um, haven't." The tailor casts a critical eye over my person. "You'll look good as a girl," he pronounces. "Thank you," I hiss. "No, You will," he insists. "You've got the face for it — small nose, jaw not too butch. And not too much muscle either. You'll be amazed what we can do with you." He stands back and surveys me with narrowed eyes. "Yes! . . . shortish wig, sort of Shirley MacLaine thing, and nice big wide-open lashy eyes . . . You'll look great, girl!" he trills. "I am not a girl," I growl, counting to ten. Obviously this is neither the time nor the place to make too big a thing of it. The tailor snorts with laughter and gives Patricia (who, if he wasn't Marie Antoinette in his previous life, evidently intends to be her at the Christmas cabaret) a sidelong glance.

The evening goes relatively smoothly. A very handsome American man who used to be a model falls in love with me and gives me his number. Apparently he has an amazing car. I play it very standoffish, but can't help hanging onto the number just in case I decide I fancy him late at night one night in the throes of a sheet-ripping hand shandy. You never know.

Patrick's manner has changed. I fear he suspects that I have no intention of "giving it up", to use the intolerably vulgar American expression.

A girl who sort of knows me from somewhere is at one of the tables with her boyfriend. We have great fun at first and she asks me all about what it's like to work here. I give her a tastefully censured version of the truth, not forgetting to point out that the one real problem with waiting is that the hours can be rather long, and everything depends on when the last customer leaves. We have a good old laugh about this and she promises it won't be *her* that keeps me there till 1am! Then she gets very drunk with her boyfriend (obviously in love) and they stay there till twenty past. I end up not liking her very much. The last tube is long gone and I have to wait hours for a nightbus. The nightbus comes. I get out my money and I only have a five-pound note. The driver wants the fare in coins and throws me off the bus. I walk home. It takes forty-eight-and-a-half minutes. As I go along my weary way, the *one thing* that keeps me going is the thought that when I get back it will be so late that the Swede will have gone to bed. I get in and *he's still up*, curled up on the sofa watching some useless art movie, dog shit flaking off the soles of his shoes, empty biscuit wrappers all over the place, crumbs, apple cores, coke cans everywhere. Both the sinks in the kitchen are piled high with skyscrapers of washing-up, and there are mouse-droppings on the floor. Added to which, the house looks really dirty. Black despair looms. Only the thought that tomorrow I have my interview with the Shafter Press keeps me from running a warm bath, getting in with my illustrated biog of Burt Lancaster, and slashing my wrists.

Up at eleven. Glorious day! I leap out of bed, sail down to the kitchen and laugh all the way through doing Bjorn's washing-up. Delicious breakfast (small cube of cheddar — only thing left in the fridge, matey!) — then sail out of the front door. Crisp wintery air and bright sun casting long shadows. I feel excited, elated, sure that something special is about to walk into my life, like the man in *West Side Story* who had an orgasm every time someone said the word "Maria". I feel sure that somewhere out there is my handsome man, and when I meet him his name will have exactly the same effect on me.

On the tube I prepare myself carefully for my interview at the Shafter Press. This is one gig I am determined not to blow. I remind myself of how uniquely suited I am to the position, in that

a) I am a bona fide same-sexer, and

2) I have, unlike so many of my brothers in this Army of Lovers which we surely are, attained the blissful state of Identity

Integration. I am therefore able to handle even the most explicit of visual material without batting an eyelid.

3) I have a deep and abiding love of literature, which may well come in handy should they ever want to publish some text alongside the photos.

I am a little nervous as I ring the bell. The house is in a residential street off the King's Road and looks rather nice. The door is opened by a not-bad-looking guy with orange hair, who gives me a look just blank enough for me to feel I should explain myself. "Um . . . I've come about the ad," I mutter, ". . . Second Assistant Editor . . ."

"Oh yes," he replies. "Follow me."

I follow him up two flights of stairs to a small office. I note that everything is very new and smart and generally "for real" looking. So much for Eric's comments about me getting a seedy job working for some gutter porno outfit. You can always tell a lot about a business from its offices (I know, because I did a lot of reading about business management once, when I was considering going into PR) and it is quite evident that the Shafter Press is on the up-and-up. The guy with orange hair makes a call to someone in another office, and then tells me to follow him again. We go all the way down the stairs again and out into the street and into the next-door house. Then we have to go up two flights of stairs again and into another (very buzzy) office, where I am politely shown a seat. Everything looks very respectable I must say, like the office in the background of a current affairs TV programme or something. Everyone looks very up-and-coming and some have even power-dressed. I don't know why, but I had vaguely expected there to be pictures of naked men on the walls, but there aren't. Just very no-nonsense year-planners and stuff. Loads of phones. One entire wall of the office is taken up by a gi-normous computer, which I am told is a sort of mega-answering machine. The company also runs those phone-in date-line things, you see, where you leave a message and then later get connected up with the man of your dreams (I don't think!) Apparently that's where all the money is. The mags — *Shafter* and *Jock-Strap* — are more of a sideline really, done for the love of it more than for the money. The manager just felt that it was wrong that there should be all that wonderful Fifties and

Sixties same-sexer porno lying around and never seeing the light of day. His motives were more philanthropic than anything else. And hats off to him, if that is the case, that's what I say!

The man who's doing all the interviewing has my application form on his desk and suddenly I feel hideously nervous. We banter for a while about unimportant things like money and prospects and then he explains that he wants to have a little think and then interview me *again* in ten minutes or so. I am beside myself with excitement. The only explanation must be that he is teetering on the brink of appointing me Second Assistant Editor of the Shafter Press. "Take Mr Carnegie" (Mr Carnegie!) "into your office for a few minutes, Ted," he tells the man with orange hair. "Tell him a bit about the job. I'll buzz you."

We go back down the two flights of stairs and out into the street and back into the next-door house and up the two flights of stairs again and into the first office. "Well, the job's pretty simple, really," says Ted — soon to be my new workmate! — "All you have to do is —" At this point the phone goes and Ted flies out of the office. Minutes pass. But I don't care. I am ecstatically planning my resignation speech for when I give up my job at Van Rijn's, and wondering whether or not to stay for the cabaret now that my next job is assured and my only reason for staying would be an unimpeded view of Bibi's bronzy thighs. More minutes pass. It becomes apparent that I have been forgotten. Resourceful as ever, I decide to use my time as a forgotten interviewee constructively. (You can tell a business graduate because he will always do this. Not that I'm a business graduate myself, but that's how you can tell them.) I peek outside the door of the office and ascertain that there is no chance of anyone bursting in on me without first clomping up two flights of stairs. Then I drift over to the filing cabinets and cautiously tweak one open.

Soon my pulse is racing and I am wondering what drug I must have been on when I got the ridiculous idea that I would be "completely comfortable" handling visually explicit material. The filing cabinet is *choc-a-bloc full* of black-and-white photos of attractive young men, oiled up, leather-capped, cowboy-booted, leather-jacketed, whip-brandishing, manacled, you name it — all united by one factor, namely that of being unclothed between the waist and the knee. Thirty gallons of adrenalin roar into my bloodstream as the filing cabinet disgorges its innumerable sanguine treasures. My hands fumble stupidly, photos fall to the floor. Trim waists, mantelpiece butts, slick quiffs, neat circumcisions . . . "Comfortable" indeed! Not only do my trousers no longer fit me by any stretch of the imagination, but also I can hardly breathe. My head is spinning. It is quite, quite clear to me that I could no more be Second Assistant Editor at the Shafter Press than Hamlet, Prince of Denmark. I slam the filing cabinet shut and pause to draw breath. Suddenly the office looks all dull again, all respectable and up-and-coming, like a current affairs programme. It seems hard to believe that the very gates to heaven and hell can have been accessed with such casual executive ease.

I notice that each drawer has a label on the front, and on each label is a date. I had unwisely plunged straight in at the deep end, 1958 — widely acknowledged among same-sexer circles to be the very pinnacle of the evolution of the fleshly male. The dates go from 1955 to 1989. Now that my pulse is becoming regular once more and my mind is clearing, I reconsider the whole matter of the cabinets. It occurs to me that the material they contain must be of absolutely priceless documentary value — to think that thirty-four years of changing tastes in homoerotica are contained in this one office! Ever the business graduate and seeker after knowledge, I decide to plunge back into the fray, motivated solely by my abiding addiction to research. I tell myself that this time I will try to retain a little distance from my subject-matter — not take it personally — just approach it as an anthropologist would.

I get through the Sixties relatively unscathed, and have no difficulty in skipping whole drawers between '71 and '77. But then things start getting to me. 1982 contains a man for whom I would willingly crawl to China, and by 1985 I am in need of a strong cup of tea and a basin of cold water. I look at my watch. I have been forgotten for twenty minutes now. I cannot believe that they will leave me alone in the office for much longer. Added to which, I am beginning to fear that my research may leave me unable to speak or even walk downstairs, and then where would I be? So I decide to do a very quick skim through '86 to '89 and then politely take my leave.

Big surprise in 1988.
Whole photoset of Eric.
For a moment I am too dumbfounded to think. I stand frozen in the sleek office, transfixed to what I hold in my hands like a rabbit by a serpent charmed. Six 10"x8" prints of Eric, completely naked, revealing absolutely all. In a way they're sort of artistic but they're also pretty smutty too. One is a back-view and the other five are hot-makingly frank snaps of Eric's reality — verging on the hard, in one case. Luckily for us all there are no props, and — vibes be praised! — no duo-shots. I really don't think I could have borne it if he had been captured on film scaling the steep cliff-faces with (for the sake of argument) some guy in a Batman mask.

This is all I need. My flatmate is effectively up there on stage, to be gawped at by anyone with a spare £3.95 and the nerve to get *Jock-Strap* down off the top shelf. In a flash I realize that something must be done. Looking nervously over my shoulder I slip the photoset into the pages of my copy of the *New Statesman* and close the drawer. I don't care if Eric signed a consent form, I don't care how much they paid him — I can't let it happen!

I run furtively down the stairs and slip out of the front door. No one notices me leave. In a way I am relieved but I am also a tad put out that the editors of the Shafter Press found me so eminently forgettable.

Once home, I pace about my room like a caged animal, not knowing what to do with the photos. They are burning a hole in my copy of the *New Statesman*! I wonder whether I should talk to Eric about them, and if so, whether it would be a confrontational scenario or not. I can't seem to be able to work out *what* sort of scenario it might be, so I resolve to keep the whole thing to myself. So Eric will never know I saved him from public disgrace. I can live with that. Better than the disgrace itself, which would surely radiate outwards to include the entire house. Suddenly I remember what Eric said about stripping for an Equity card, and I gasp with shock. Could it have been true after all? I sit down on the side of my bed, the sobering realization dawning on me that perhaps I know my flatmate a lot less well than I thought I did.

One thing is for certain, though: I have to find a place to put the pics before I leave for work. I try everywhere — under the bed (with my back-numbers of *New Statesman*), in my underwear drawer (where I keep my drugs), stashed in with my records. But each place seems perilous. What if someone comes into my room looking for drugs? Or a record? Or a back-number of *New Statesman*? I curse myself for being so hippy-like as not to have had a lock fitted onto my door.

In the end I settle for the temporary solution of hiding them under my pillow, working on the assumption that no one would be so foolhardy as to rootle about in such a potentially yucky neck of the woods. Isn't that where people keep snotty hankies? I know I do.

I go downstairs and indulge in an organic peanut butter sandwich (yes I know, Tookie, I know, but I've bought the pot now, haven't I?). I am just settling down with the toxic but tasty feast when the doorbell goes. I sigh. It is of course rather important, if you are a waiter, to get at least *five minutes'* peace and quiet before you go out to work.

I open the door.

It is Barney.

Part Two

INDEPENDENCE CELEBRATIONS

SIXTEEN

After many years of having made the humanoid race the object of my closest scrutiny, I have been reluctantly forced to the conclusion that *man is not by nature a particularly tolerant creature*. In fact, quite the reverse! How many wars have been fought in the name of religion! what injustices perpetrated under the tawdry flags of race and class! what energetic vendettas pursued by family upon family! — and so on. Quite how the humanoid has managed to acquire for himself the reputation of being a "social animal" shall always remain an impenetrable mystery to me, for most of the people I have met in my life have displayed an uncanny tendency to judge their fellows rather harshly — to hate them first, indeed, and then think of an excuse for doing so afterwards. I would even go so far as to suggest that this is the very principle upon which our "society" is founded. But forgive me — I rave.

I make these no doubt very banal observations, however, in the spirit of the greatest humility, holding myself to be by no means the least of sinners in this respect. I have upon many occasions been guilty of intolerance, I admit it. I am perhaps a *leetle* less hog-snarlingly bigoted than this country's main contribution to postwar culture, the lager-lout, but that is probably because this is my eightieth life. I am by no means perfect. If I were, I would by now have been assumed into the Light, my individuality lost forever in one eternal moment of is-ness. I would be, in fact, a sunbeam.

I was never particularly tolerant of Barney, for example. I was quick to criticize him at every available opportunity, and skilled at crushing him in arguments and ridiculing his taste. The fact that he remained my friend for as long as he did seems to me now a glowing testimony to his sweet and affectionate nature, and I can't help feeling nagging twinges of guilt when I think back to all the times I made him feel small. I think perhaps it was his expression that made me do it — it was a sort of "ill-treat me" expression, similar, as I have said before, to that of a bloodhound. I was young, and I did what came naturally to me. I ill-treated him.

I *do* feel rather bad about this now, that I cannot deny, but the funny thing is I still can't really think of Barney as, well, *cool* I suppose — and this is intolerance. No other word for it. Barney is a lovely person, God-loon or not, and I should be ashamed of myself. One thing I can say, though: I think I can trace this intolerance of mine back to its source. I have thought about it a lot, and I believe that my real stumbling-block with Barney is the fact that *I know he wears Union Jack underpants*. A classic example, I suppose, of intimacy breeding contempt — for if I had never been allowed to rootle around in his clothes cupboard in search of Wolfgang records I would never have known the way things were beneath his corduroys. And I mean never. Designs on Barney's person have never been entertained by either me or my organs of (ha!) procreation, so you can put that one right out of your mind. Added to which, Barney is straight as the driven snow, or so one assumes.

The last few times I saw Barney there was already a great yawning gulf between us. I had lost my virginity more thoroughly than a man ever should (if the somewhat selective modern Christian readings of the Bible are to be believed), and he, of course, had not. For a while I tried to go on as before — a room at my aunt's, Wolfy-and-Vesta sessions round at the old bloodhound's — but I knew it couldn't work. I felt like a vampire. I felt damned. I knew that I must either go the whole hog or turn back and repent, right there and then, before the life-boat of Salvation bobbed irrevocably away from me as I floundered about in the warm waters of the sins of the flesh. I need hardly add that I could no more turn back than transform myself into a ravening tyrannosaur. I didn't even try.

I went back to the house in which I now live and, on some shallow pretext of having left something behind upon my previous visit — my prayer-book perhaps — rang the bell. Eric opened the door on this occasion, but Corey was in too, and we had a lot of fun introducing ourselves to each other. (Interesting note here: I have often observed that Eric and Corey seem quite blissfully unconcerned about meeting people with whom the other — usually Corey — has *already* enjoyed carnal relations; it is only when extra-marital hanky-panky is *in the offing* that things can get a little tense.)

"Eric, this is Lenny," chirped Corey, making tea; "Lenny — Eric, my boyfriend."

"Oh," I blushed, totally out of my depth. Talk about in at the deep end! Not only was this my first (knowingly) all-same-sexer tea-party, but also I was being required to revise my whole naive map of the twilight world of love. So this was what they meant by the sexual revolution! I felt like stout Cortez.

"Don't be embarrassed," crooned Eric serenely, deliberately spooning six spoonfuls of sugar into his tea. "Corey and I have an *open relationship*. He's told me all about you." Big, tolerant grin. What a guy!

"Well . . . that's all right, then," I husked, staring fixedly at my shoes. I was at this stage under the impression that Corey's reports back to Eric were thorough and detailed — a theory which I now question — and that therefore Eric knew of the precise manner of my Fall. My ears burned like volcanoes.

"Are you from round here?" Eric politely inquired, maybe sensitive to my delicate post-virginal state and ever the gentleman.

"Um . . . Chiswick . . . I stay with my aunt," I confessed.

"And what's that like?"

"Well, it's not too far from the tube, but the trouble is, the Piccadilly Line only stops there in rush-hours," I babbled.

"No, I meant, *does she let you bring guys back?*" Eric patiently explained.

My ears exploded into fountains of white-hot lava. "Um . . . no," I croaked. "In fact I'm looking for a place of my own somewhere. Maybe somewhere . . . nearer the tube . . ."

I moved in a week later. And I can't help thinking back to that first tea-party, now that the wheel has, if you like, turned full-circle, and I'm the one who lives here and Barney's drinking the tea. Well, not quite full-circle, of course. I'm sure Barney has still managed to hang on to all the many virginities which Scripture advises the Pilgrim to keep on ice. Anal, oral, intellectual . . .

Come to think of it, why *is* he here?

For a while we banter of this and that, as one does. I tell Barney of my life as a pillar of the alternative community, and he confirms my previous guess that he was working his way thrustingly up through the ranks of the tellers at Barclays. Married, too! Patter of tiny feet (one, eighteen months, boy). Attaboy, Barney! Souls for God's kingdom! I wonder whether he still wears Union Jack underwear, but it's been a few years and so I put the question on a back-burner. Perhaps if I slip some dope into his tea it could be like the old days and we'd have almost no secrets again. And then again, maybe not. Barney looks about the house, trying to think of nice things to say about it. There is of course virtually nothing nice you can say about our house. "Love the mouse-droppings!" — "Great simulated thumb-print wallpaper!" The poor boy is obviously turning these and other options over in his mind and wisely plumping for nothing but an all-inclusive, vacuous smile of approval.

"Still see your aunt in Chiswick at all?"

"No . . . not at all, actually."

"Oh."

"I'm pretty busy most of the time, what with the restaurant and stuff."

"I suppose you must be."

Pause. We both look at the mouse-droppings. ("Yes, I thought they were rather *chic* — picked them up at Conran's don't you know — marvellous gimmick — latest thing! Got them all over Channel 4 apparently!")

"Church?" I venture.

"Yup."

Grins. Blushes. Barney looks like he has something on his mind. Come on, Barnes me old mucker, spill the beanz, I won't bite!

"I saw your dad the other day," he announces at last.

Silence.

Nothing can be heard but the moist phut phut phut of shit hitting the fan.

"*You* saw *my* father."

"Yes."

"*You* saw *my* father."

"Yes. He . . . um . . . came round."

I look at Barney in disbelief. My feelings churn within me. I had really thought he had come of his own accord. In my infinite naiveté.

"He suggested I came round to see how you were doing," ventures my guest.

My feelings curdle. "Well that does seem rather a roundabout way of carrying on," I quaver. "If he has something to say to me he can always pick up the telephone." (Note: the monologue is my father's preferred mode of discourse. He has never rung me since I left home, though he has kept up a fairly regular stream of didactic prose communications.)

Barney looks at the mouse-droppings. He is doing his best to be diplomatic, poor boy, but he doesn't really stand a snowball's chance in hell, the way things have evidently been set up. "I think he actually feels a bit shy about ringing . . ." he starts.

"*Shy?*" I cry. "*Shy?* His letters aren't shy, I can tell you that! Not unless you'd call Moses shy when he came thundering down Mount Sinai, smashing up the first draft of the Ten Commandments . . ."

"But fathers are always like that, don't you think?" says Barney, pulling out all the diplomatic stops. "They bluster about, but deep down inside they're just little boys like all the rest of us . . ."

"Little boys indeed!" I rant. "I've never heard such a preposterous load of rubbish in my life! I'm — I'm very, um, upset about this whole thing, Barney. I thought you'd come round to see how I was doing —"

"I did, but —"

"No you didn't, you came as a lackey. A — a *lackey*. I'm . . . I'm . . . *outraged* . . ."

"Sorry."

Long silence.

"Do you want me to go?"

"Um . . . yes."

"OK."

Barney goes.

I sit in the dirty room and stare at the empty mugs. I feel betrayed. I go up to my room. I walk round my room. I put on my tape of transmissions from Planet Fargon via the divine W.A.M. I turn it off again. I lie down on my bed. I think of my parents and suddenly I am heaving with hot tears of rage and self-pity.

"Why didn't they love me?" I sob. *"Why didn't they love me?"*

SEVENTEEN

I pull myself together and go to work. The American ex- model comes in around ten. Table for one. He cleverly fixes things so that I wait his table. Ho hum.

He's really good-looking, actually, though a little older than I might normally plump for. Strange thing is, I don't think I fancy him — the old juices just fail to flow. Ridiculous, really, I know — and I deserve to be whipped from Land's End to John O'Groats for being so outrageously picky. Obviously if I saw him in a magazine he would be instant hand shandy fodder, but *the humanoid mind is a very strange thing*, and the fact is that in the flesh this guy just doesn't cut the mustard. So here I am, screaming for a boyfriend, and *turning down* an ex-model who's probably rich too and who is reputed to own the fabbest car this side of the Atlantic. He asks me when I get off work and I can't help feeling a small thrill of pleasure. To be wanted! Desired! And by someone you don't actively loathe! When I first took the job I yearned to be asked when I got off work by American ex-models, and now here I am and it's happening. I tell him it all depends on when the last customer leaves, and then wag my finger at him and tell him that he'd better not keep us all here till twenty past one or there'll be the devil to pay with brass knobs on. He laughs (quite nice smile) and says, "Don't worry, I'll be good, but can't I give you lunch one day? I'm Italian and I'll cook for you. When's your day off?" For a moment I have almost forgotten that I don't fancy him. Italian! And offering to cook! My head spins, and I blurt that my day off is tomorrow, but that doesn't mean I'm free for lunch, and anyway I'm not really in the mood for dating guys right now, sort of on the rebound, no offence I hope. Then I beat a hasty retreat, thinking to myself, Rebound indeed! If I'm on the rebound then it must be from a steamy affair with a handsome centipede in my last life, cos I sure as hell ain't never had anything worth rebounding off in *this* one!

The model guy leaves around eleven without importuning me further. I must say I appreciate good manners in a man. In fact I've heard it said that *manners makyth man*, and my studies have confirmed this to be the case. The last customers leave around midnight, and after a lightning clear-up I leap out at ten past, hot on the trail of the last tube home, a rare luxury. I could be tucked up in my cold lonely bed by half past, and stoned by twenty to! Just as I am getting to Earl's Court a fantastic sky-blue Cadillac draws up alongside me, all chromium and red tail-lights, like something out of *Lost In Space*, and I realize it's Greg, the ex-model. He asks me if he can give me a lift. A lift! I stand on the curb, mesmerized by the car, unable to speak. Then after a while I say something about how kind it is of him to offer but I really can manage very nicely on my own. This little declaration of independence apparently makes him all the hotter. He asks me where I live and before I know what I am saying I have coughed up the details.

"Oh, come on, Lenny, I'm not gonna eat ya!" he grins. "Let me take you for a little spin — no strings, I promise. What's the use in having a nice car if you can't share it with people you like?"

His logic is absolutely irrefutable, and also he has been extremely gentlemanly and delicate on the subject of *strings*, so I get in with a shy smile and say, OK then, just to Hammersmith, I must say this is very kind and it *is* a totally fabboid car. As we sweep through the streets I am beside myself. The suspension lurches and sways in a fashion not wholly unerotic, and all the interior is in sky-blue and chrome. We arrive at Hammersmith and he asks me if he can cook me lunch tomorrow and I say yes and he says he'll pick me up at twelve, and as he drives off I think to myself, I sure hope the other guys in the house are there when he picks me up! Then I stop myself. What an outrageously smooth operator! I don't even want to go out with him and I've said yes already! Then I tell myself not to be such a tight-ass, and what harm can one little home-cooked Italian lunch with a dreamboat do?

Next morning I am in such a good mood as I contemplate being picked up by Greg in his fabulous car that — as if to celebrate — I tell the pesky Swede, straight out, to do his washing-up for once. His reply is a model of teeth-grinding hypocrisy: "Yes, Lenny, you are right. I was going to do it last night, but I got to bed so late — I was watching a fascinating film from Poland — quite hard to understand but I do have very advanced powers of concentration and I know a lot about films. It is indeed vitally important that each of us does his own washing up at all times, otherwise how can we all live together *higurnically*? It must have been very difficult for you to force yourself to bring me up on this point but you were quite right to and I'm glad you did. In return for this favour I shall not hesitate to do likewise, should you ever forget to do yours."

I consider pointing out that it might get done quicker if he spent less time making speeches about it, but I am in such a good mood that the thought just flits through my mind. I actually feel like having a chummy chat with the old swine.

"So how's your sex-life?" I chirp, nestling down with a copy of *New Internationalist*. (Note: my motives in bringing up the subject of sex-lives are not entirely selfless, as I know that I shall soon be picked up for lunch by a very jealous-making package.)

"Funny you should ask that," he replies. "I met a guy just last night. I think there is a little spark, perhaps. I'm not sure. I think I feel something. My feelings are so complex. But the one thing I can say for him is, he does have rather a nice car."

I smell blood. "Oh, really?" I ask casually, flicking through the *N.I.* "What sort?"

The Swede chuckles dismissively. "I'm actually not particularly into material things," he pronounces, with a smugness that makes me want to leap up and throttle him, "and I do think it's rather shallow when you hear these guys rattling on about their boyfriends' cars — as if it was the car they were sleeping with! But still, it has to be admitted, his car is nice. And rather expensive, too, I suspect. It's a BMW."

My sense of impending victory swells within me. A BMW indeed! But I need my triumph to be unqualified, so I lead him on further. "Sounds lovely! I suppose it must be quite roomy, and have a tinted windscreen and so forth?"

Bjorn smiles the shy little smile of the boy who is being serviced by the hottest stud on the block. "It's quite a big car, yes," he blushes, toying listlessly with the washing up. "Not that I care, of course, but it is quite big."

Just at this point Greg pulls up outside our house in his enormous sky-blue Cadillac, tooting the horn and waving handsomely out of the window. I look up as if surprised. "Oh! Is it twelve already?" I trill. "Well bless me! That'll be my lunch-date! See you, Bjorn!" And I sweep out of the house.

I cannot resist looking back as we pull away in the dream-car. Bjorn is looking out of the window, ashen-faced, a defeated man. I luxuriate in the glory of the moment.

We get to Greg's flat, which is sort of small but really swishy. It's actually done up rather tastelessly, but I remind myself that it is important to be very forgiving on taste matters with anyone who came of age in the Seventies. On one of the walls is a big painting of Greg lying back on a bed with his shirt off, looking like one of the Bee Gees, and I feel my powers of forgiveness being stretched to their absolute limits. But soon we are laughing and chatting over a delicious lunch of spaghetti and salad and cheese and stuff, and Greg tells me all about his family and shows me snaps and stuff and talks about Italy and the little house they have there up in the mountains, and I can't help thinking how absolutely wonderful it would be to be his boyfriend. I mean, I'd be able to drift around at parties at his side and know that he was the handsomest man there and everyone was jealous! We could drive all over the place in his sky-blue Cadillac, making every pedestrian in London jealous! We could jet off for little holidays in the Italian mountains with his mum and very beautiful sister and cousins and things, and we could all sit round at a big table like in a Bertolucci movie and eat brightly-coloured vegetables and fruit, and black local wine, and have the best time a couple of boys could possibly have. I look at Greg and try to force myself to fancy him. I have another glass of wine.

After lunch we have a fun time looking through scrap-books of photos of Greg when he was a model, and I find myself drawn into a philosophical musing on the subject of the hand shandy and its meaning in our lives. In the pictures Greg looks unforgivably beautiful, the sort of man that makes you want to nail yourself to barn doors and dig up the body of your dead ex-lover! I wonder how many sheets have been ripped in homage to his pictorial image the length and breadth of the western world, how many tons of washing powder consumed in the wake of a zillion spurted tributes to his loveliness! And here I am, actually beginning to feel a little bored by all these wonderful pictures. I quite obviously deserve a sound thrashing for my perversity.

After a bit, Greg suggests a walk down Portobello, and we step out into what has developed into another glorious winter's day. We nip into Mr Christian's to-die-for delicatessen and buy some olive-bread and then somehow it's time to leap back to Greg's flat to enjoy it with jam for tea. Then, amazingly, it is movie-time, and it just seems to be that sort of day so I can't really say no when he proposes it. We go to see a fascinating film about a robot who likes to shoot people in the testicles, and afterwards enjoy a quick half in the Champion in the best of spirits. I glow with pleasure in the knowledge that I am on a date with the best-looking man in the whole place. Then it's back to Greg's place for just a smidgeon-widgeon of fab Italian wine and a few laughs, by way of nightcap to round off what has undoubtedly been a most enjoyable day.

As soon as we get back to the flat I realize we are approaching Danger Point. I know Greg is a complete and utter gentleman, and I'm sure he doesn't necessarily expect us to perform sex on our first date, but hey! we both know that this is the twentieth century and long engagements kind of went out the window during the Blitz, so there is a *leetle* tension in the air, that cannot be denied. As I sip my wine I try to concentrate on all the yummy pictures of Greg that made you want to grab him and ball his brains out, but, amazingly, it doesn't make any difference. It must be something to do with his vibes I suppose. We all have vibes and some vibes just don't match with other ones. A friend of mine said it's do with skin. Apparently we all have skin (well, obviously) and everyone's skin has a different sort of electronic charge to it, and if your charge doesn't like someone else's charge, then you just don't fancy them, and no amount of looking at pictures of them will make any difference. They could have the top half of Tom Cruise and the bottom half of Mel Gibson (tell me about it) and you just wouldn't care. Ah life — life!

As the clock strikes twelve I get up and thank Greg very politely for a fabulous day and explain that I must be on my weary way. He very chivalrously insists on driving me back to the house, and all in all we get over the difficult part of the evening without too much trouble.

I go up to my room and am about to go in when I notice a note pinned to my door. This is what it says:

STOP! DO NOT GO INTO YOUR ROOM!
Dear Lenny — I have taken the liberty of giving Barbara your room, as I was pretty sure you'd be staying the night with that great-looking guy who picked you up for lunch (NB: if you didn't you're even stupider than I thought). We have been working on <u>Private Lives 2000</u> all day and the poor thing was too exhausted to go home. If by any strange chance you do come back tonight you can share my futon.
— Eric.

I am speechless with fury. That I should have been betrayed by Eric of all people! Not only am I furious, but also shocked. There seems to be an idea developing in the house that my room is in some undefined way "up for grabs" to any old carthorse who's too lazy to catch their night bus. I storm into Eric's room.

"I'm — I'm — outraged!" I splutter.

"Here," he replies, handing me a very large spliff.

I take a toke. It is strong shit alright. "Eric, there seems to be an idea developing in the house that my room is—"

"I'm sorry," says he. "I thought you were going to sleep with that nice-looking guy you went out with . . ."

"Just because I have lunch with a guy, and just because he may have regular features and a nice car, it doesn't mean my underwear is as good as removed," I snap. "I mean, it was a first date, you know — but I don't suppose you stopped to think about that, did you? You just assumed that my room was in some way —"

"Oh, for heaven's sake, Lenny, I've said I'm sorry."

At this point the dope starts to take hold.

"Holy shit!" I mutter, and get into bed. Just as I am slipping away into a dream-filled oblivion I remember that I left the photoset of Eric under my pillow . . .

EIGHTEEN

Morning. Or something very like it. I wait till Barbara *deigns* to come down for breakfast, picking her way delicately through the mouse-droppings and empty cereal packets that lie about on the kitchen floor, and then I dash up to my room. I look under my pillow. The photos are still there. I take them out of the envelope and count them.

Five.

I count again.

Five.

One rear view, four from the front. Am I going stark staring mad, or were there six when I got them home from the Shafter Press? No, I am certain there were six: One of his, um, back, and five of his, um, front. Suddenly I remember, with horror, that there was quite definitely one photo in which Eric's reality was verging on the hard — it was, to be sure, the most hot-making by a long chalk — and *it is no longer here*!

I sit on the floor of my room, stunned, trying to work out the significance of this dreadful news. Someone has stolen a picture of Eric in a state of mild excitement — but who? Who, apart from the obvious person, of course? But I cannot seriously believe that Little Miss Mind-the-Mouse-Droppings has actually slipped one into her real leather executive-style attaché case! The thought is just too ... too ... Who else has been in my room? The Swede? One of the other people I've never met who live in the house? Eric? I realize with a horrible sinking feeling that it could have been anyone. Little Mr Trusting with no lock on his door! Little Mr We're-All-One-Big-Army-Of-Lovers! I crossly curse myself for my ridiculous naiveté. I consider going to Eric for advice but somehow I just can't face it. I would have to confess to having gawped at his mildly excited reality, and no, no, I'm afraid I simply lack the programming to deal with that one. We're probably terribly old-fashioned in many ways in this house, I mean I know a lot of people in maverick establishments leap about in the nude the entire time, but we tend to keep our private parts to ourselves here. That's just the way things have worked out, and, hung-up though we no doubt are, these unwritten conventions have a habit of being rather difficult to break. Shit, shit, shit!

I whop on the Big M's fortieth — slow movement — and lie down on my bed — or at least, the bed which once was mine but which now seems to be common property. I implore the spirits and the vibes to send me inspiration. How serious is this ... this *leak*? Exactly who is the photo going to be passed on to? Will it be reproduced in any great quantity? After a while my mind begins to clear. I remind myself that things could hardly be worse now than they were before I found the photoset in the files of the Shafter Press, rolling slowly but inexorably down the conveyor belt towards publication by the grimy million. But on the other hand, things are also rather worse, in one crucial way, namely this: if the pics had been published in *Jock-Strap*, they would merely have been gawped at by (with a bit of luck) a few million people one had never met and never would. But now ... now ... Barbara Honigsbaum has one! Barbara Honigsbaum has *the dirtiest one*! For some reason I am absolutely certain, with every fibre of my being, that Barbara has stolen the photo. And this certainty brings with it an undefined, inexplicable sense of doom.

The Big M's penultimate symphonic slowy chugs and thrusts its way through those miraculous old chord-changes, and my vibe-centres drink in new strength from the heavenly transmission. New resolve. I realize that there is only one thing for it: I must somehow try to get the damn thing back. I fly downstairs in the hope of finding Barbara's briefcase unattended, only to see her swishing out of the front door chirping something to Eric about their next read-through, briefcase in hand. Damn! damn! damn! I stomp into the kitchen and put the kettle on.

Caffeine is soon offering me another chance at optimism. What we now face, I tell myself, is the rather delicate problem of trying to get access to *Barbara's house*. Tricky one. If one could get her to invite us to dinner . . . Some hope! She's already been round here for food just grillions of times, and shown absolutely no signs of offering to reciprocate. I rack my brains. There has to be an answer!

The phone goes. It is Barney. I'm so cross with Barbara that I completely forget that I'm supposed to be cross with Barney, and we have a very nice little chat. He says he's sorry if it looked bad, him coming round with a message from my Dad, but the fact is he did want to see me, and is he forgiven? I say, Of course, Barney, of course, no hard feelings me old mucker, let's meet up. Lunch? says the bloodhound. Why not? I chirp. You can come round in your lunch-hour and I'll throw a salad together. (Barney's bank is really just round the corner, you see. How can I not reopen diplomatic relations when this is the case?) Barney says that actually he's already had his lunch-hour (I notice with surprise that it is half-past-two) and so we fix a date for tomorrow.

Amazing. Barney and I get on like something closely resembling a house on fire. Maybe a house *quietly smouldering*, or a house *in which someone has just thrown a lighted cigarette into the kitchen dustbin before going to bed*. But anyway, we have a few laughs. I can't help feeling that it is rather fun to have a friendship with someone who is in so many ways *on the other side of the great divide*. Perhaps we can have fun teasing each other about our respective "lifestyles". Perhaps he'll be on for a few nights out on the fab same-sexer circuit. You never know. Eric says there's nothing more soothing than going out with docile heterosexual men — they are so appreciative of the humblest little manifestation of our maverick culture, all you have to do is take 'em down the Royal Oak on Amateur Drag Night and they react like they've just witnessed the Virgin Birth. I wonder whether Barney might enjoy some time off from holy homemaking as a day-tripper to Sodom. I put it to him. Far from screaming the place down and running a mile, he is very polite about the whole idea and obviously just a little bit intrigued. We arrange to meet up on Friday and take in the mud-wrestling at the City Apprentice. Funny to think that Star of the Future Barbara Honigsbaum wasn't up to this one, but Pillar of the Patriarchy Barney Barrett is.

"I'm not so sure about Barney," says Eric. "I'm not so sure."

We are sitting in the First Out, husband-shopping for me, infidelity-shopping for him, lingering over our bean-sprouts. There are some *very* intellectual-looking types here today — some are even reading books! I must say that strikes me as the height of cool, to read a book in a place where everyone else is up to their necks in serious cruising. To read a book! I can't deny that I am extremely impressed. Occasionally the guy (it's one guy in particular who's getting my juices flowing, though there are two of them reading books) pauses awhile as if transported by the words on the page, sighs and looks up vacantly, obviously miles away (*I don't think* — the little cheat is actually packing *all his cruising* into these moments) and at such times he will let the cover of the book sort of spring upwards a bit so that you can almost see what the title is. It's a real tease. I am by now absolutely desperate to know what the book is, and each time he flashes the cover I manage to glean about one more letter of the title. So far I know the first word is "The", which sort of narrows it down a tad.

"What do you mean, not sure about Barney?" I probe, disappointed. "I thought he turned out rather well."

"Oh, I like him a lot," says my flatmate. "What I meant was, *I have my suspicions* . . ."

I pause, perplexed. Eric smiles knowingly. "Oh, come on," I say at last, "you don't mean . . ."

"I'm not saying anything at this point," says he. "I just thought he gave off vibes, that's all. He seems pretty interested in the mud-wrestling."

I am flabbergasted. "Well, I must say that possibility hadn't occurred to me," I muse, "but then you never can tell. Did you really get vibes?"

Eric nods sagely. "I reckon I did."

I ponder. "But he has a wife and a baby!"

"Nevertheless."

"Well, I'll be doggonned!" I conclude.

"I may be wrong," he concedes.

"Probably are."

"But I may be right."

"We shall see, I suppose," say I.

"We may."

"Shall we invite him to my party? And his wife?"

Eric snorts with laughter. "Well, that would probably depend on whether you intend to be hiring Rick to let you feel him up in the middle of the sitting-room or not."

"I thought we'd been through that," I huff. "You've already poured about twenty gallons of cold water on the whole sleaze idea, so there's no need to take the piss."

"It's your party," says he; "you're in the driver's seat. I was only commenting."

You will have noticed that the party idea has *not* died a death — thank God! Which is amazing, really, because every time the subject comes up I get very snappy and cross. I'm not sure why. Obviously the idea of filling the house from top to bottom with eligible same-sexers is an absolute must, not to mention my only hope.

"Maybe we should phrase the invitation so that he doesn't feel obliged to bring his wife," I muse.

"You never know, maybe *she's* a swinger," says he.

"Well, if they both are, the God Squad must be a lot more fun than it was when I was a member," I note, stirring my fennel tea.

"Let's give Barney a time to get used to us and our radical lifestyle," says Eric. "Then, if he seems to be taking it all in his stride, we can invite him to your husband-finding. After all, we don't want a phantom at the wedding-feast, do we?"

"A what?"

"We don't want Barney sitting there in the corner radiating scared vibes and spoiling the party spirit. I mean, sleaze or no sleaze, there could well be a bit of tasteful groping going on, and if he's going to have hysterics then he'd be better off staying at home."

"You're so right."

"So what we do is, we see how he likes the mud-wrestling, then maybe we try him out with a smidgeon of drag, and after that maybe take him to see Rick at the Phoenix—"

"Wouldn't that be a nadger on the sleazy side?"

"Well, yes it would, but of course no one would be groping him—"

"Who, Barney?"

"No, Rick. Generally the audience doesn't get to grope the strippers at the Phoenix, and also, it would be a key moment for Barney observation."

"Expand."

"Well, Rick's an attractive young man. I think we can safely say that if there is so much as the merest nadger of same-sexer orientation in our subject, it will manifest itself in some subtle fashion when Rick takes his shorts off."

"You could say that about the mud-wrestling too, though, couldn't you?"

Eric muses awhile. "Hm," he concludes. "The trouble with the mud-wrestling is that, challenging though it is, it might work as aversion therapy."

"Hadn't thought of that."

"I mean, the guys who go in for it can be pretty horrendous sometimes."

"There was a lovely guy last month . . ."

"Exception."

"Maybe you're right."

Eric finishes his tea conclusively. "Here's my game-plan: skip the mud-wrestling—"

"Skip the mud-wrestling?"

"We'll go another day. Start Barney off with some soothing drag — something not too challenging . . ."

"Amateur Night at the Oak?"

"Amateur Night would be ideal. We don't want some psychotic Amazon in a twelve-foot wig singling out members of the audience for special humiliation. If he's still on for laughs after Amateur Drag Night, we take him to see Rick. And watch him closely at every stage."

"Sounds like a marvellous plan."

Serene little smile. "I must say I get a vibe . . . Maybe he could be the answer to your problem . . ."

"Leave it out Eric," I sigh. The mere thought of carnal relations with Barney makes me feel very strange and yucky. It would be like incest.

NINETEEN

Next day is a funeral, worse luck. Our dear friend Steve, recently carried off by the Big A. I go with Kenny. We get to the church, and I peep through the doors. There's this doomy music playing and people standing round looking lost and somehow I can't believe we're in the right place.

"Go on," says Kenny, "go in!"

We go in. The atmosphere is just terrible. I catch myself thinking, *This is like a funeral!* then I realize that it *is* a funeral — my first, to be accurate.

"I wish this was all over," says Kenny.

I tell him so do I.

Interesting note about Steve's funeral: Steve's family came, but *John's family* (John is — was — Steve's boyfriend) didn't. I must say I thought that was a bit much. I mean, if one of them had been a girl and they'd been married they'd have come, wouldn't they? Oh, parents! What are we going to do with them?

Barney says I've got to "make my peace" with my parents, as he puts it. I say, What about them making their peace with me? It's them that banged their Bible and said same-sexers won't go to heaven. "That's not the point," says Barney. "The point is, you're a grown-up person too, now, and you have just as much responsibility to forgive them as they you."

I pause. I must say I have never looked at it that way before.

"Listen," says Barney (we're in that chi-chi fake-French bistro place on Hammersmith Broadway), "the fact is, you not speaking to your parents is going to be a continual drain on your spiritual energy — or vibe-energy or whatever you want to call it. It's like if you went out and left loads of lights on in the house. Even when you're not thinking about it it's draining you. It's a fact. You can't deny it."

I push bits of red cabbage round my plate and huff in exasperation.

"It's alright for you," I pout.

Silence.

"Maybe it is," says he at length. "But you should at least think about it. What about your brother and sister? Don't you want to see them?"

I start to feel very funny and cross. "It's not my fault," I mutter.

"You could write to them. It might be a way back."

"My dad likes to protect them from real life," I tell him. "He makes me feel like a vampire."

We sit and watch the people walking past.

"How long has it been?" says he.

"Nearly four years."

"You should go and see them."

Hammersmith Broadway. Fleshpots. Babylon.

"All this bitterness . . ." says Barney. "It'll eat you up."

We finish our lunch and Barney goes back to Barclays Bank for another half-day of thrusting. I stand in the street, still feeling funny and cross. I decide to walk down to the Wholefood Emporium to cheer myself up. I get there and I remember I once had tea in the cafe in the back with the beautiful Asian boy who had a boyfriend all the time, and this just makes me feel funny and cross again. I buy a bag of carob-coated raisins and some smoked tofu (well, you only live once) and walk down to Ravenscourt Park. Lie on my back. It's warm for winter.

As I lie looking at the sky it occurs to me that in many ways it's rather presumptuous of people to have children at all — to get the idea into their heads that they are together enough to bring them up. It's a funny old world, and no mistake. All these people thinking they know better than their kids, and filling their little innocent heads up with rubbish, and then getting cross with them when they go off to become mavericks and things. I wonder whether I would have procreated had my juices flowed to the sound of a different Pavlovian gong, and decide that yes, I probably would have, and yes, I probably would have filled my little children's heads up with all sorts of silliness. I then realize with horror that if I had not been a same-sexer I would probably never have seen through the God thing — I would have been exactly like Barney! I shudder at the thought and decide to go home and comfort myself with the smoked tofu.

I get back and Greg calls. He knows it's my day off. He rang Van Rijn's. I am sort of outraged but also rather flattered. He asks me out to drinks at his place followed by dinner somewhere nice. My immediate reaction is to make excuses, but because I haven't properly prepared myself for this conversation — I suppose I was vaguely hoping that if I ignored the problem it might just go away — the excuses aren't very convincing, and they buckle under the weight of Greg's persuasive, cheerful charm. He really is lovely to talk to on the phone.

He picks me up and we drive round to his appallingly decorated flat. He pours me a drink: really nice malt whiskey. I haven't had it for years. He has bought me a present. My heart sinks. I unwrap it. It's a shirt. It's actually rather nice: dark blue with little white bits. He asks me to put it on. I go into the bedroom and come out looking very smart in it. He surveys me beamingly.

"It looks really great on you, Lenny!"

I feel like an impostor.

We drive into town. Everyone looks at the car. We leave it in a multi-storey and walk into Soho. High-class Chinese place. Beers, fab food, funny Chinese wine stuff. I thaw out a tad and stop worrying about the end of the evening. Greg makes a couple of remarks about there being no strings. He's so polite, and I really wish I wanted to sleep with him. I start worrying again. It's not that he isn't a perfect gentleman — he is — it's just that it's so obvious he's in love with me. I feel I shouldn't be there. You know how it is when you're in love with someone and you're convinced that they're just *ideally suited* to you — you think you can sort of persuade them to love you. You think you can make them see the logic of it. But the trouble is, of course, you've gone mad. *Because you're in love* you're forgetting all those nitty-gritty truths about the push and shove of the world between the sheets. Greg has forgotten all those truths. I, unfortunately, have not.

We go back to his place for another lovely malt whiskey, and a quick gander at another scrap-book full of pictures from when he was a model. He certainly seems to have an endless supply!

I ask him to drive me back to my place, which he does. Suddenly the tricky part of the evening is upon us. End of the second date: Moment of Truth, by *anyone's* calendar (except maybe Jane Austen's). Greg makes a very polite move for his goodnight kiss. He gets one, but the wrong sort. I flee.

I get into the house and go to my room and feel terrible. The evening has made me feel terrible. The whole day has made me feel terrible. I look at my clock. It is still early. I'll never sleep. I pace about my room, trying to think of a way to knock the day on the head, preferably one which doesn't involve the Burt Lancaster biog, the bath and the razor blades.

I knock on Eric's door. He's out.

I go downstairs. The Swede is in the sitting room, feasting on some no doubt very *higurnic* frozen meal. (His hygiene-fetish, or should I say *higurn*-fetish, has led him to the strange position of only eating food which has been previously frozen and preferably irradiated too. I have tried to explain the rudiments of nutrition to him, but my words have fallen on deaf ears. When I make nut cheese he is convinced that I am trying to poison myself and looks at me as if I belong in a mental hospital).

I go back to my room again. I lie down on my bed. Going out with Greg has made me feel even lonelier than before. I suddenly realize in a blinding flash that if I don't go to bed with someone within the next twenty-four hours I shall explode. I get out my address book and feverishly leaf through its pages, looking for those special phone numbers that pulsate and throb in that undeniable way that phone numbers do when they mean sex. I can only find one. It belongs to Yogesh, the beautiful Asian boy who I had an affair with but who had a boyfriend all along. I ring him up. It's been rather a long time and at first he doesn't really know who I am. But then he remembers and says, Hey Lenny!

It's been so long! And he very sweetly invites me round to have dinner with him and meet his boyfriend. This wasn't really what I had in mind — I was sort of envisaging an almost entirely non-verbal encounter consisting of only him and me — but somehow it's impossible not to accept the invitation, what with me having rung in the first place. I put the phone down and hiss an inchoate curse.

I go downstairs again. I reflect that the Swede is, theoretically at least, a human being, and so I decide (misguided hippy that I am) to attempt to enjoy his company for a while, by way of getting through the remainder of the day.

The attempt fails. It was doomed from the start.

We start to watch a movie together. It is a fascinating old classic about a little boy who is in fact a fiend in humanoid form. As the opening titles roll, Bjorn makes himself extremely comfortable (shoes on) on the sofa, and brushes crumbs and cold peas covered with tomato ketchup off his pullover and onto the floor.

Then comes his voice. His voice! Bark, bark bark! Yap, yap, yap! I grip the sides of the straight-backed chair I have been kindly allowed to sit on and concentrate on the idea that he is a fellow member of my race, not some beast sent from hell to torment us all.

"Yes, this film is going to be very interesting," he barks over the crucial opening lines of dialogue. "Very interesting indeed. I wonder how they are going to do this. The whole thing of demonic possession. Hm. It is a subject I have studied in some depth. I wonder if they are going to be able to transfer it to the screen. Somehow I fear not. But I'm willing to give them a chance. Let's see how they do . . . hm . . . no. . . no, this is *not* good. . . no, this is very bad . . . I would have done it quite differently . . ."

I realize that he intends to bark and yap his way through the entire movie, and so I politely take my leave and go back to my room. If I wanted to have my movie barked over I would go to a pet-shop and buy myself a dog. At least it wouldn't expect me to take it seriously.

I lie in bed and think of Greg. I think of his inexhaustible supply of pictures of himself, and the thought occurs to me that, though he looks fab, maybe he is a profoundly boring person. Perhaps my vibe-centres picked this up before my conscious mind did, and sent a message down to my organs of uncleanliness, warning them not to get excited. Maybe this is why I can't get it up for the guy.

I go to sleep. I dream of my family. I dream of my brother and sister.

TWENTY

On my way round to Barbara's pad, I wonder why it is exactly that I feel this overwhelming sense of dread at the thought that she has stolen the picture of Eric. No matter how hard I try, I cannot think of anything she might do with it that could justify the terrible vibe the whole thing is giving me. She could show it to her chi-chi friends. They could laugh. But ultimately all that would prove is that we were living on the edge, whereas they were not. I mean, they would be to some extent challenged by the photo, even if they didn't admit it. What else could she do? Show it to *our* friends? She doesn't even like our friends. Have it printed on a T-shirt and wear it to parties? Somehow I can't really see it.

I am on the tube. I have a cassette in my pocket. I am putting Plan A into action. Plan A goes like this:

1) Wait till Barbara is round at our gaff rehearsing *Private Lives 2000* with Eric and Tookie;

2) Go round to Barbara's gaff and hope that her flatmate is in;

3) Get access to her room on some flimsy pretext.

4) Get the photo back.

The pretext I have chosen is that I just happen to be in the area, and Barbara has particularly requested to borrow my compilation tape of Wolfy's slowies (sort of true) and I just *happen* to have the tape on me, and so I thought I'd drop in and drop it off; furthermore, Barbara once said I could borrow her *Atom Heart Mother* (also true-ish) and so I was wondering if I might just pick that up as a sort of exchange. In this manner I hope to gain a good couple of minutes alone in Barbara's room, supposedly rootling through her record collection, but actually hot on the trail of stolen porno.

I ring the bell. Barbara's flatmate opens the door and asks who it is. We haven't met before. I tell her I've come by with something for Barbara. Is she in? The flatmate says Barbara's not in but I can come in anyway. We go up some stairs, and Barbara's flatmate banters of this and that in a carefree fashion. We get on like a house on fire. She is a blonde bombshell, actually much prettier than Barbara, only she obviously hasn't been told that this is the case because it doesn't seem to have occurred to her to become a star. We introduce ourselves. She's called Josie and she's from Australia. She makes clothes. I go through to her room and there's a sewing machine and stuff and just loads and loads of the most incredible gear. Very Ken Market/Portobello, if you know what I mean, but really kind of up-market too. Apparently she's going to have some stuff in a feature in one of the colour supplements real soon. I am thrilled. Some of her stuff is for boys and she lets me try it on. I look marvellous. It's all very baroque and frilly and just a smidgeon pervy too for good measure. Josie says that I should really consider commissioning her to make me some made-to-measure knock-'em- dead outfit, it really wouldn't be very expensive, she'd only charge me for the materials and the time. I say, How much? She says, Well, what do you want? I pick out a very minimalistic sort of outfit and Josie says, Lord! that wouldn't cost a penny more than £200! My jaw drops open and I remember that I am in the presence of someone who is, of course, by her very nature as one of Barbara's friends, on the chi-chi side of the street. I have a good old laugh and say, Josie me old mucker, it would take me about two years to save up £200 the way things are right now. You are talking to a bona fide member of Thatcher's underclass. I'm afraid I'll just have to love your stuff from a distance. Then we have tea, and I realize that anyway I could never have worn the gear to the Royal

Oak, and even if I had it would never have got me a husband. (Note: same-sexers like to think of themselves as terribly fashionable, but most are thoroughly conventional in their own way. It is unwise to draw too much attention to your clothes if you wish to have a sporting chance of making "new friends". Speaking of which, whatever happened to Corey's "new friend"? I must say I haven't seen hide nor hair of him since the hellish trip back from Brighton. One can't help wondering whether the old cliff-scaler managed to pull off the full three-lemons-in-a-row routine or not. Indeed, now that I think of it, I can't help feeling that if there is a vampire in this story it can be none other than His (ha!) Toothsomeness, in that, like The Count, he surely comes and goes as if incorporeal, nipping into the house when no one's home, making use of our kitchen facilities and then disappearing as soundlessly as he came. This, of course, is only my personal theory, but then I *have* done my homework and I know what I know.)

I give Josie the old *Atom Heart Mother* story and ask if I can nip into Barbara's room, confident by this time that I have won enough of her trust to get away with a good five-minute rootle. Josie tells me that's fine in theory, only Barbara — can you believe this? — has had a special lock fitted to the outside of her bedroom door, and she locks her room when she's out. I am flabbergasted by this news, and ask Josie if she doesn't find this flatmately behaviour a tad, well, ploppy I suppose. I mean, what does Barbara think Josie is? Josie patiently explains that it's all to do with insurance. Barbara has a lot of rather expensive jewellery apparently, and you can only insure stuff in a rented room if you have a lock fitted on the actual door of the room. I am relieved to hear this explanation, but also, of course, well narked that my glorious Plan A has fallen flat as a pancake. I go home racking my brains for Plan B.

Luckily the old brain-cells seem to be experiencing a renaissance of sorts, because by the time I surface from the tube Plan B is fully formed. I must say I am rather proud of it. It's complicated, but then, so is the design of the internal combustion engine, but that didn't stop it from revolutionizing our lives, did it? Plan B goes like this:

1) The main object of Plan B is to get access to Barbara's flat

when Barbara is there, and her room therefore unlocked.

2) The idea of trying to *hint* Barbara into inviting us round to dinner is pure cloud-cuckoo-land: the old frump obviously has no intention of ever lifting a finger to entertain us, beyond the possible donation of a cigarette to make a joint (out of dope which we have paid for).

3) What we — I mean I (Eric can have no hand in this) — have to do is this:

a) Find a movie which is playing near Barbara's and which is almost definitely going to be sold out. Tricky, but not impossible. Barbara lives very near the Fulham Cannon, where things often get pretty busy.

b) Make sure all the other movies showing at the cinema are really bad, so there is no second choice.

c) Persuade Barbara to go out to see this movie with us. What then happens is this:

i) We get there. It's sold out. Big downer. Everyone looks at the other movies showing. They're really bad.

ii) Black cloud descends upon the party. Evening looks like complete failure. *What can be done?*

iii) At this point I pipe up: "Just a minute! I happen to have a tiny smidgeon of Leb on me! Why don't we pick up some beers and go back to Barbara's gaff? It's really near, isn't it?"

d) Barbara cannot refuse. Indeed, she won't want to, drug-pig that she is.

e) We go back to Barbara's gaff and have a marvellous time. Maybe Josie's there and we don't have to get bored out of our skulls talking about *Private Lives 2000*. I ask to borrow Barbara's *Atom Heart Mother* and she's too stoned even to get up, so I leap up and say, I'll get it! Mind if I rootle through your collection?

It can't fail. Also, I'll have more or less as long as I like, because time means nothing when you're stoned and someone's rootling through your room. They could be in there for an hour and a half and you'd just think there'd been a time-warp.

Soon Amateur Drag Night comes round, and blow me down if Barney isn't round at our gaff all freshly scrubbed and suitably dressed as a lumberjack. We give him dinner — baked potatoes and butter, lots of different cheeses, salad and fruit. Whole thing costs about £1 a head. Marvellous stuff! Unfortunately, we were unable to fix things so that Bjorn would be out — you can't win 'em all — and so what could have been an absolutely delightful meal is a little marred by the old woof-woof routine, but it's new to Barney, and he thinks it's rather a laugh, bless him. Come to think of it, we all thought Bjorn was a laugh at first.

Greg calls while we are having dinner. I put him off. Damn! damn! damn! Why is life so complicated? You spend six months trying to find a boyfriend and the next six trying to get rid of him.

Then we troll down to the Oak in high spirits. Eric and I are excited about starting our Barney-observation programme. We feel a bit like Richard Attenborough. On the way we tell Barney that same-sexer bars are absolutely nothing to be afraid of — his virtue is quite safe, no one's going to bite, etc., etc., etc. Of course, these assurances just make Barney all the more tremulous and scared, not unlike a small furry animal. Maybe they even make him all the hotter, but time will tell on that score.

The show, is, as ever, completely mind-numbing. What happens on Amateur Drag Night, you see, is that these guys get up on stage who have obviously thought about dressing up as ladies and doing playback on a tawdry wooden stage (yes, the stage is back) for absolutely ages. They have taken about ten years to work up the nerve to actually do it. So they go to the Royal Oak on a Tuesday, give the DJ a tape of their favourite song, and WHAM! suddenly they're up there, dressed in clothes usually associated with the female of the species, supposedly lip-synching to their favourite song, and *they suddenly realize they don't know what they're doing*. They usually come to this realization somewhere between the end of the first chorus and halfway through verse two. Either way they're left with a good two minutes of wandering about the stage like little lost lambs, cruelly exposed and sweating through their clownishly daubed face-paint. Woe betide the first-time drag who plumps for a 12" dance-mix! I've seen it happen, and, believe you me, it's not a pretty sight.

Obviously, if your only experience of entertainment is what this Police State, in its infinite mercy, has seen fit to beam down the cathode ray tube, you're going to find Amateur Drag Night disorienting, to say the least. Well, it is. It challenges your every preconception of the thin line between fantasy and reality, ritual and art, cruelty and entertainment; it is at once a gloss on and product of the state of alienation in which we live, quite apart from its more complex semiotic valencies. But I digress — more of this in my book, *Irony and Self-Oppression on the London Same-Sexer Circuit* (currently slightly bogged down in Chapter Two).

Barney stands there like a small furry creature, clutching his half, his big melancholy eyes darting from the face of one potential ravisher to the next, insanely over-sensitive to the most minute glances and gestures. I encourage him to drink up, putting it to him that if he doesn't chill out just the merest nadger he's not really going to have much fun. Beer flows freely, drags come and go, Barney loosens up, Bjorn barks.

As the effects of the old alcohol take their dastardly toll, I am struck with an incandescent perception. I realize that Bjorn, for all his avowals to the contrary, is perhaps one of the most materialistic people I have ever met. He loves marketing. He loves cars. He lusts over deep freezes and yearns for increased levels of irradiation. I begin to wonder whether he might not get along rather well with Greg, who is, after all, more of a product than a person, and I think it is really a product rather than a person that Bjorn needs. The glory of it! If that were really the case, I could get Bjorn and Greg off my hands in one fell fiendish swoop!

By the time we leave Barney seems to be glowing with fulfilment. He very sweetly thanks us for an eye-opening night out, and we go our separate ways.

"Next stop, Rick at the Phoenix!" says Eric, once we are out of earshot.

TWENTY-ONE

Next day is a General House Meeting to discuss, among other things, the matter of the hazelnuts. Eric is very hopeful that we might at last have managed to tie down everyone who lives here into coming. I am feeling very businesslike, and so I clear the kitchen table and find the Minutes Book and a biro that works, and I lay them down in the middle of the table so that they look very official. I stand back and survey the effect. Good. Then, in a fit of inspiration, I get the pot of hazelnuts and put them on the table too. Exhibit A, as it were. I cannot resist having a tiny peek inside to see how the little colony of disgusting unidentified insects is getting on. Inside the tupperware pot things are looking rather like a scene from that marvellous film about aliens leaping out of people's stomachs. The colony of critters seems to have died — suffocated, one would guess, by the no-nonsense efficacy of the airtight tupperware design — but they have left behind them a scene of decay and metamorphosis. Half-eaten hazelnuts lie about, mixed in with the dry corpses of the doomed banqueters, and all has been partially covered in a sort of furry web. Everything is the same colour: grey. All in all, extremely Ridley Scott. I hastily close the lid and put the pot back on the table. I wonder whether I should make little nut cheese nibbles but decide that that might be a bit over-keen. This is, after all, a House Meeting, not a wedding reception.

In the event, the only people present are Eric and myself and a charming young guy who I have never met before in my entire life, but who insists that he has been living on the third floor (in the room next to Tookie's) for the past six weeks. He's from Wales and seems to go by the rather odd name of Mice. That's his name. Mice. I point out that there are some small *unhigurnic* rodents living in the house who have sort of bagged that name already, and won't it get rather confusing if he insists on using it too? Mice just laughs and says that's never been a problem up to now. I say, Yes, but have you ever lived in a house with *actual* mice before? He changes the subject at this point, obviously very attached to his outrageous name and not really wanting to negotiate.

"OK, then," says Eric. "Shall we begin?"

We all sit down round the table.

"Members present?"

I sigh in exasperation. "This is exactly what I mean. What's it going to look like in the Minutes Book?"

"What's what going to look like?" says Eric.

"*Members present: Eric, Lenny and Mice*," I sigh. "I'm sorry, but people will think we were taking the piss."

"But it's my name!" says Mice.

"Nevertheless," I tell him. "Nevertheless."

"It's his name," says Eric.

"Well don't come crying to me when everyone else in the house stops taking House Meetings seriously," I warn.

Sharp cynical laugh from Eric. "Apologies for absence?" he asks, pointedly.

"None received," I reply.

The meeting doesn't take long. The fact is you simply can't get anything really important decided unless everyone turns up.

But anyway, it has been fun meeting Mice at last, and to celebrate making friends we all go up to his room for tea. We go in, and from the looks of it he does seem to have settled in — maybe he really has been here for six weeks. He's got a little dope-farm going with a sun-lamp and everything, and photos of his boyfriend on the walls and stuff, and new furniture from

Camden Lock. Apparently Mice is an unconventional young designer who is about to shake the fashion world to its very foundations. I must say the clothes he's wearing are absolutely splendid. Extremely girlie, but you can get away with it if you're in fashion I think. The afternoon just flits by, and before I know it it's time for me to go to dinner with Yogesh and his boyfriend.

I crossly get ready and go out. It seems a foregone conclusion that the evening will make me extremely depressed. Yogesh lives about twenty grillion miles away, in Hackney. As I sit on the tube I reflect that the dinner had better be bloody good, considering how long it will have taken me to get there, combined with the added consideration that what I want will almost certainly not be on the menu. I find the house and am introduced to Yogesh's boyfriend. He is called Gavin and seems very friendly. Not exactly my type — physically I mean — but I can't see that there is anything to stop us from becoming chums. (I must say I like my men about six feet tall and pretty muscular too, with not an ounce of fat on 'em — *ideally*, that is — though I know that I am asking for the moon here. Gavin is lovely but has plumped (forgive me) for the fuller, more Falstaffian figure). Yogesh and Gavin banter away very fast of nothing in particular, and it is impossible not to detect a note of shrill hysteria in the proceedings. I politely return the banter, inwardly pondering the meaning of these matters. It seems that between me and the more highly evolved members of the humanoid race — of which Yogesh and Gavin are obviously two examples — there will always remain a yawning gulf. I shall never understand highly evolved psychology. I mean, why all the nerves now, after all the frankness earlier on? ("Hallo Gavin? It's Yogesh here ... yes ... Hi! I'm round at Lenny's and I'm going to stay the night ... OK — Bye!") Why now, after Time has run its supposedly healing course?

I remark upon the loveliness of their white carpet and they say, Yes, isn't it lovely, we can't have parties, you know, because our carpet is so lovely and we're afraid that someone might spill red wine on it. We all have a good old laugh about this, and soon dinner is served. Spaghetti bolognese. And why not? Yogesh dishes up the fab munchies, and in the process knocks over the bottle of red wine. Instant hysteria. The carpet will never be the same. We get a good half-hour's value out of this little crisis, by the end of which my sympathy is beginning to wear a *leetle* thin. Why have a white carpet at all? that's what I say.

By the time we have got to the pudding course I am beginning to have ghastly suspicions as to source of the evident hysteria. The distinct possibility looms that not only is Yogesh *on the menu after all*, but *so am I*, and — and here's the tricky bit — *so is Gavin*. We are all on the menu. We are going to be served after the coffee and before the cigarettes. Of course, it's only a hunch, but you know how it is when you get a feeling about these things. You're usually right.

After dinner coffee is served and we look through some slightly yawny albums of Yogesh and Gavin's holiday snaps. I fear the worst. Only a host whose judgment is being put under some considerable strain will bring out holiday snaps, unless they're really amazing. I mean, they'd have to have Prince Charles in them, really, wouldn't they, or the Dali Lama at least, or someone less famous but with their trousers down. We finish the snaps and suddenly Gavin gets up and, without any sort of explanation, goes through to the bathroom and has a shower! My heart sinks. Yogesh is indeed looking lovelier than ever, but I have always had real problems about going to bed with people who turn me off, and, try though I may to persuade myself otherwise, old Gavin seems to have fallen ker-plonk into the old thumbs-down category. I'm sorry, but there it is.

Ten minutes later Gavin returns in what can only be described as a nightmare of a dressing-gown, and I realize that the time has come to tear myself away before the next course actually emerges, steaming, from the kitchen. They both seem terribly disappointed that I have to be going so early, but I point out that I do live in Hammersmith, etc., etc., etc., and you know how it is, etc., etc., etc. As I walk out into the cold Hackney air I reflect that the evening has been nothing less than a complete disaster. I get home and it's still too early to sleep.

I go into my room and go over my Plan B for getting back the stolen picture of Eric. Everything is set for Friday. Then it occurs to me that maybe I should take a quick snoop round the pesky Swede's room — little Scandinavia, as I call it — on the off-chance that it was after all him and not Barbara who did the crime. My instincts tell me otherwise, but you never can tell. I tip-toe up to his door and give a polite little knock. Nothing. I try the door. No lock. I go in.

Inside it is a hell-hole indeed. The place is just piled high with clothes and empty biscuit wrappers and books on marketing and magazines about cars and deep freezes and things. And on top of all this, like snow, is a layer of loose sheets of paper. I pick one up. It is Bjorn's CV. I pick another up. I realize that *they are all Bjorn's CV*, but all are slightly different, with words crossed out here and there and paragraphs inserted and deleted. Suddenly I feel like Shelley Duvall in that chilling movie when she reads Jack Nicholson's novel and realizes that he's been writing one sentence over and over again for the past eight weeks. Bjorn's CV is complete drivel, drivel subjected to a hundred painstaking revisions and refinements.

"I have travelled much," I read, *"and in the course of my travels I have found myself in a hundred-and-one unexpected and sometimes even quite dangerous situations, like Harrison Ford in <u>Raiders of the Lost Ark</u>. But somehow I have always managed to survive, whether by sheer good luck or by dint of my native Scandinavian wit, and my experiences have matured and ripened me like a fruit . . ."*

With a sense of dread and foreboding I realize that I am standing in the presence of madness, and I reel stunned from the room. If the photo of Eric is in there, I'm afraid that is where it will have to stay, because I for one don't want to be around when Bjorn starts hacking through the door with an axe!

TWENTY-TWO

Everything is planned. At the Fulham Cannon is another film about a robot who likes to shoot people in the testicles (it's the latest craze), and everyone is very wound up and excited about it. I have ascertained from Patricia at work that the film is sold out nearly every night, and today is Friday, so we haven't got a chance.

"But do you really think we'll get in if we don't get tickets in advance?" says Eric.

I breezily brush the objection aside. "Patricia went last Friday," I tell him, "and apparently it wasn't very full."

The evening has sort of snowballed. Initially it was going to be just me, Eric, Barbara and my secret lump of Leb, but now there's going to be Tookie and Corey and maybe Barney too. Let's hope the whole thing doesn't blow up in my face. Naturally I can't let on to any of the others that it is in fact a fiendish plan and we're not really going to see the movie about the robot, at least not if I have anything to do with it, so I have decided that my best course of action is just to brazen it out as if I were innocent as the day is long. I have to make it look as if I really am on for it. I have therefore generously offered to cook baked potatoes for the entire posse before we leave, and have even invested in a small lump of cheddar to help the potatoes slip down. Obviously we must establish a genuine party-vibe if the thing is going to transfer smoothly to Barbara's pad when the movie part of the evening falls flat.

I spend the afternoon in the delightful task of sending out invitations to my party. Nothing fancy — just plain white postcards with the time and place etc., etc., etc. Somehow I feel that's more exciting than mucky xeroxed collages of cuttings from *Playgirl*. And no silly theme either, like *everyone has to wear shorts*. I once went to a hopelessly yuppyish same-sexers party where everyone had to wear shorts. I really genuinely believed that maybe I would meet my future husband there. Little did I know. Everyone was sweeping about the place in shorts talking about the stock market. I got a lift home with some bankers in their car. They were saying, "Yes, marvellous idea of Justin's to throw a shorts party. Just what I needed really. Got back from the office today feeling pretty knackered, you know — just wanted to collapse in front of *The City Programme*, but then I thought to myself, No dammit all, I'll go to Justin's shorts party — and I'm glad I did!"

I leap out to the post-box and whop my invitations in. It is another glorious day.

When I get back I put up a big notice in the house inviting everyone, and Tookie sees it and gets terribly excited. She asks if I am going to invite any straight men (the poor dear has been looking for a boyfriend for almost as long as me) and I say, Yes of course Tookie, would I forget you? even though actually I hadn't been planning on it up till then. I rack my brains to think of some straight men I could invite. Bibi springs to mind, but I am doubtful about the wisdom of such a move. He is beautiful and he is friendly, but on the other hand the whole Bibi thing has a funny vibe on it that seems to be able to go either way: sometimes it makes me feel good and sometimes it sends me bolting for the razor blades. (Added to which he is Mediterranean, and, though one would assume he's basically OK with same-sexers, you can never be sure with these guys. He does work in Van Rijn's, and — incredibly — he does live in a room in the flat of my loathed employer Patrick, but still, you never can tell. Maybe he's secretly planning the perfect anti-same-sexer crime and is going to poison the soup on his last day there. Forgive me — I rave.)

Tookie asks me if I knew that the date of my party was the same as the date of Barbara's birthday. I say, No I didn't actually, does that mean the dear thing won't be able to make it? (Fingers crossed behind back!) Tookie says that as far as she knows Barbara hasn't got anything planned for her birthday, so in a way it's rather nice that my party is that day, because at least it means the poor thing won't be on her own, feeling all unloved. Perhaps, says Tookie very politely, obviously not wanting to appear out of line, perhaps it might be a nice idea to maybe even get a cake in, you know, just as a surprise. She won't be expecting it at all, and it'll be so nice to see her little soon-to-be-famous face light up! I say, What a wonderful idea, Tooks me old china! Barbara shall have a cake! We can all whop in a couple of quid get a really nice one! But not a peep of this to the birthday-girl, mind! We want this to be a surprise! Later on I get a little nagging twinge of doubt about the Barbara/cake idea. I know it's silly, but I sort of feel funny and cross about it. I mean, one minute it was my party and the next it was Barbara's. But I tell myself not to be such an old scrooge and get on with the much more important task of making sure there are going to be lots of handsome same-sexers there. Obviously I must use every single spare minute at my disposal between now and the party *networking*. Otherwise I will have only myself to blame if the thing is dull as dishwater.

Barney rings and says hi, and he *is* looking forward to coming out to the movies with us, but he's got rather a lot on, and he thinks he might have to miss the baked potatoes. I say, Fair enough, just be here by eight-fifteen and we can all go together. Barney says, OK, and if I'm not there by eight-fifteen just go without me and I'll meet you at the cinema. No problem! I chirp. The whole thing is getting terribly complicated, but I'm afraid it will just have to run its course now. One of the big pluses so far is that there's absolutely no sign of the pesky Swede. With any luck he'll be out somewhere in his new boyfriend's roomy BMW, or maybe doing a spot of late-night window-shopping for deep freezes and vacuum cleaners. It seems extraordinary that Corey is coming, but then on the other hand he has done this before: he'll say he's on for it and then change his mind. Presumably it's got something to do with the workings of the hormonal system in highly evolved people. I think they get to seven o'clock or so and then undergo a sort of metamorphosis, after which the very idea of the cinema pales into insignificance compared to the prospect of a brisk hike across the Heath. Be that as it may, we all eventually find ourselves seated round the venerable old kitchen table by the romantic light of six white candles, happily cracking beers and tucking into our simple fare. Let others dine on caviar and champagne. We simple mavericks can make do very well without, thank you very much. We know, you see, that there is more to life than swishing about being rich. Indeed, at the backs of our minds is the awareness that many a rich bastard would dearly love to enjoy the sparkling wit and razor-sharp dialectic of our humble table — would gladly exchange a month's supply of caviar just to be allowed to chew on our discarded potato-skins, if only we'd include him in on our groovy scene. Actually, we don't discard the skins, of course, because that's the most nutritious bit, but you probably know what I am driving at. Let the rich bastards howl outside our big front door. They have their reward. Let them eat cake.

Everything goes pretty much according to plan, right down to Corey undergoing his strange hormonal change and deciding not to come after all. Eric and Tookie and Barbara and I wait till eight-thirty, then set off for the cinema. Barney is no fool and will presumably meet us there. As we walk down the street I nervously finger the lump of Leb in my pocket. The photo of Eric, I tell myself, is as good as recovered.

Get to the cinema. Big bummer. Film sold out. What are the other movies? I innocently look at the other titles with my friends — yes, they're all really terrible, not a lot to pick from there! It's nine-fifteen and too late to try and catch a movie somewhere else. I keep a low profile and patiently wait for my moment. We all stand around like dummies. Corporate indecision. I count to twenty, allowing the party-vibe to drift towards the very brink of extinguishment. Then I point out, in a little tiny lamb-like voice, that I *do* have a pretty sizable lump of the most mind-blowing Leb in my pocket, and we *could theoretically* troll round to Barbara's and get blitzed out of our skulls. At this, the party-vibe floats gracefully skywards like a zeppelin and we set off for old

Frumpy's gaff. Half-hearted bleatings from Barbara about how we shouldn't go back to her place because her flatmate is throwing a dinner-party. Excuses, excuses, Barbara! We've had just about enough excuses from you, all in all. We're going back to your pad to get hog-snarling, and nothing you can do can stop us! On the way Eric buys some cans of Red Stripe, and I reflect that Plan B couldn't be going more smoothly. By ten my friends will be too stoned to move.

At Barbara's place I am pleased to find that Josie is in. She is obviously pleased to see me — even though she *is* in fact in the middle of throwing a very small dinner-party — and we have a couple of laughs. We all promise to stay in the sitting-room, out of the way of her dinner, but she says, Nonsense! I'm doing tempura — why don't you all try some? I realize she's obviously just being polite, because how the hell is she going to make a dinner for three stretch to seven? and so I very firmly say, No thanks Josie me old mucker, we've eaten anyway, we'll just sit here and quietly scale the old cliff-faces of enlightenment while you three get on with your high-class munchies. What is tempura anyway? *Don't you know?* she positively screams. Tempura is simply the most divine thing this side of Tom Berenger's bottom! It's a Japanese thing — you chop up bits of meat and veggies and then coat them in egg and stuff and deep-fry them! Mm-Hm! — That's as may be, I reply firmly, but we've all had a lovely and filling supper of baked potatoes à la Carnegie, and we really are pretty full.

We settle down in the sitting room and I roll a spliff, whopping in just loads of the Leb, and send it on its way. (NB: I pretend to take a puff but do not inhale, as I want to have a clear head for the successful implementation of Plan B). Eric cracks the Red Stripes and soon we are buzzing like a swarm of bees. Just as the dope begins to take hold, Josie serves up her tempura feast in the adjoining room, and the house is filled with sweet Japanese aromas. Suddenly Tookie and Eric and Barbara decide that they are absolutely starving, which I can understand in a way because that is one of the side-effects of the old weed, but on the other hand I can't help feeling just a nadger offended that they should be starving after I went to such lengths to provide them with what I had imagined to be an absolutely delicious and satisfying meal.

Soon they have joined Josie's table and are tucking into a dinner that was obviously only intended for three and I am sulking in the sitting-room, refusing to be associated with their outrageous behaviour. I have not forgotten about Plan B, however, and so I occupy myself gamefully in the construction of a couple more knock-out spliffs, one of which I light up and pass on to my "friends" at the dinner-table. Then I go back to the sitting room and crossly read a book of Josie's about the fashion world. It's quite good, and says that the whole thing is one enormous conspiracy. *Quelle surprise.*

Twenty minutes elapse. Josie is obviously in a bit of a flap, frantically searching through her kitchen for any spare scraps of food she can coat in egg and deep-fry, and I feel ashamed of my friends all over again. I go in and have a quiet word with her about how she really shouldn't worry, seeing as it was so rude of us (us!) to eat her party-food in the first place, but she is Adam Ant. I then breeze past the dinner-table and drop another joint in front of Miss Drug-Pig (big cheesy smile as I do so — attagirl, Barbs!) and ask if I can rootle around in her record collection for a while, maybe even borrow *Atom Heart Mother*. She is already pretty far-gone, and offers no resistance to the idea. My pulse races. Plan B, your time has come!

I go to Barbara's room and linger with my hand on the door-handle. Can I go through with it? How long shall I allow myself for my search? How stoned are they all? I look back at the dinner-table. Everyone's eyes are swollen and red, eyelids drooping lazily downwards and stupid smirks playing about their greedy lips. The third joint is on its way round, and it seems to be taking no prisoners.

"Holy shit!" says Eric, choking. Somehow one always seems to say that when the weed comes down on one like a dose of salts. People start giggling at nothing in particular. The clock strikes ten. It's now or never. I go in.

Well, life is full of surprises in the real world, and today seems to be no exception. I suppose I was expecting to have to look through drawers and things to find the photo — to at least have to make some sort of effort. Nothing could have prepared me for what I see as I enter. Not only is the photo of Eric immediately apparent — framed, and hanging over the bedstead like a religious icon — but also, there are grainy photocopied reproductions of it *all over the walls*. Barbara has had it blown up to A4 size and sort of papered her room with it. I stand in the middle of the floor, rigid with shock and disbelief. The place has been turned into a shrine to Eric in his most uncompromising manifestation. *Has the woman no shame?*

A moment later I stumble out of Barbara's room and head straight for the bathroom. No one seems to notice me. I lock the door behind me and dive for the cold tap. I put the plug in, fill up the basin and then immerse my entire head in the icy water. I come up spluttering and coughing and wrap my head in a towel. I will just pretend I was in a drug-warp or something. I'll just go back to the party and pretend I didn't even go into Barbara's bedroom at all. No one will care. No one ever cares, now that I come to think of it.

I rejoin my chums and try to join in, but you know how it is when people are stoned and you're not. Somehow the jokes don't add up to much. Suddenly I get a splitting headache and announce that, fun though it's been, I'm bolting for the stables. I get up and make as if to leave. Eric kindly offers to accompany me home and I say, No, no, don't bother, I can make it back on my own thank you very much indeed. Eric says that actually he wouldn't mind an early night as he and Barbara are going to try to make a really early start on *Private Lives 2000* tomorrow, and he'll come with me if I give him five minutes to get his shit together. I say OK and slump down into the sofa, still in the throes of extreme disorientation. No matter which way I look at it, I simply cannot believe that the woman who was too uptight to go to the mud-wrestling has adorned her room with pornoshots of my flatmate. I remind myself that the truth is often stranger than fiction, and try to focus my energies. Maybe I was wrong about Barbara all along. Maybe she was always a swinger and I never noticed. Maybe . . .

"Oh, you can't go until you've seen the designs I got Jimbo to do!" chirps Barbara as Eric rises to leave. "There's a great one of you with pointy ears!"

"Bring them round tomorrow," says he. "I'm too stoned now."

"But wouldn't you like just a tiny peek?" she protests. "I've got them in my room. Come and have a lightning gander."

I stiffen. What manner of madness is this? Barbara Honigsbaum luring Eric into her obscenely decorated bed-chamber? Has everyone gone mad? Am I in fact in some sort of drug-warp after all, high on the mere fumes of the dastardly stuff? *Am I dreaming?*

Eric follows Barbara into her room. She slyly closes the door behind them. I strain to catch their conversation, but Josie is chatting away at me and one of her friends has put on Tina Turner doing *Addicted to Love*, with the volume cranked up to a rockin' level. What seems like an eternity passes.

"*Your body sweats,*" thunders the Acid Queen, "*Your teeth ger-RIND . . . !*"

Eventually they re-emerge. I study them carefully, eager for tell-tale signs of conspiracy. Eric looks a trifle flushed. As well he may!

We leave. As we walk to the tube I can't think of anything to say to Eric. Just nothing. I rack my brain to think of something to say to him, but everything I think of just seems ridiculous. I mean, I could comment on how pleasantly mild it is for the time of year, but that would be absurd, seeing as we both now know that *the other one knows* that Eric did a softcore porno session, and I stole it from the offices of the Shafter Press. I consider jumping straight in at the deep end and saying something like, *Did you have sex with the photographer?* (the obvious question), but somehow a question like that needs to be led up to kind of gradually. Other than this, my mind is a complete blank. I decide to pretend that I am too stoned to speak. Maybe Eric *really* is too stoned to speak, in which case perhaps we will be able to get home without saying anything at all, and then we can sort of pretend the thing never happened and I never gawped at his mildly excited reality and everything is just like it used to be, all simple and nice.

Eventually Eric gives a little snort of laughter. "Really, Lenny," he says; "you are too much."

I swallow hard. "Am I?"

Eric snorts again. "Yes," he says. "You are."

We walk on for a while.

It seems that the cat is now more or less out of the bag, so I decide to thrash it out. "Well, what was I supposed to do?" I quaver. "Just leave them in the file and wait for them to get published?"

"I dunno," rasps Eric. "I dunno . . ." Then he snorts with laughter again.

"Why are you laughing?" I snap, feeling very left out of it, what with one thing and another.

"No reason," he slurs. "I'm just stoned."

We walk on.

A couple of minutes' silence. Then another snort. This really is intolerable! I refuse to be the object of some nasty little conspiracy, when I have gone to such enormous lengths to spare Eric from public humiliation! "What are you laughing about?" I bark, my sense of humour deserting me entirely.

Eric grins widely, his eyes narrowed to little stoned slits. "I just think it's so funny that you actually made her pay for it, that's all."

"That I did *what*?"

"That you made her pay for the picture. I just think that's hilarious." Another snort.

I am outraged!

"What has that woman been telling you?" I thunder, or at least, attempt to thunder. I am probably still sounding like a small furry animal crying for its mother, but let that rest.

"Forget it, Len," says Eric. "I just think it's funny, that's all."

"*She stole that picture, I'll have you know!*" I cry, now quite beside myself with rage. "I put it under my pillow, and *you*, in your infinite wisdom, generously gave Barbara my room, and in the morning *it was gone* . . ."

"Yes, Lenny, yes, I believe you," says Eric, unsuccessfully attempting to suppress a grin.

"Well, do you or not?" I cry. "Because I for one do not particularly want to go on living in a situation where trust has broken down . . ."

"Calm down, Len, I believe you."

"No you don't—I can tell!" I splutter. "What's so fab about her that makes her word better than mine?"

"Nothing, Lenny. I believe you."

We walk on. Silence. We board the tube. Eric sits trying not to grin, but it is apparent that a little half-smile of amusement is playing about his lips. I do not sit beside him but stand up all the way, looking out of the windows. I am absolutely furious. Apart from anything else, he should at least be *slightly* embarrassed about pictures of his willy being on general release, but I cannot detect so much as a hint of decent shame.

We get back and it is still pretty early. We are still not speaking.

As we walk down the hall my attention is partially caught by the sight of a pair of Union Jack underpants hanging on the fox head, but I am too cross with Eric to take it in.

We go into the kitchen. Corey and Barney are there. Neither of them is clothed.

Barney is bent over our venerable old kitchen table, and Corey stands behind him, a look of supreme concentration on his face as he ploughs his way into the fleshy mysteries that lie between Barney's dazzlingly white and surprisingly curvaceous buttocks.

TWENTY-THREE

Hideous embarrassment. Corey stops what he is doing and looks up. Barney looks up. For a brief moment both evolved and under-evolved are united in a general breakdown of *savoir-faire*.

"Um . . ." says Eric.

We withdraw.

Eric wisely closes the kitchen door.

We stand in the hall, both of us (I think) wondering what options lie open to us in the circumstances. Going into the sitting-room may or may not be advisable, as we have no way of knowing whether or not the door that connects the sitting-room to the kitchen is open. I look at the fox head. Time stands still.

"I think I'll be off to bed," Eric announces.

"So will I," I agree. It is obviously not the time for cocoa and biscuits.

We go our separate ways.

I reflect, as I drift off to sleep, that it has indeed been a most eventful and difficult-to-assimilate day.

Next morning I get up at lunchtime, and am just enjoying my coffee when Greg calls. This time I am ready for him. I politely wriggle out of his fervent proposals of evening amusement and then come back at him with my ace card, namely inviting him to my party. This seems to have the desired effect of calming him somewhat, and as I put down the phone I tell myself that he will soon be out of my hair for once and for all, when I link him up with the pesky and deranged Bjorn. Well, one can but hope. When the Swede himself appears in the kitchen I make sure that he has got my invitation and is planning on showing up. It is fairly apparent that he is not in a position to turn any party-invite down, and so I relax in the certainty that, if no one else turns up, Bjorn and Greg will be there, and Plan C can go ahead with all guns firing.

As I am toying with a little brunch — beansprouts, *homegrown, NB* — I am joined by Tookie. I notice that her hair is now bright blue.

"Lenny," she starts, in a tone which implies she has something on her mind.

"Yes, Tooks me old china?" My tone is light and morningy, even though it is, strictly speaking, the afternoon.

"Well, I know you're probably going to think this well out of order," she chirrups, "but I was *just wondering* . . ."

I give her a matey grin. "Spill the beanz!" I chuckle.

"Well, I was just thinking about your party," she spills. "And I was *just wondering* whether it might possibly be OK for me to invite a few people . . ."

I beam broadly. "Of course!" I tell her. "No need to ask. Are they handsome?"

Tookie chuckles apologetically. "Well, actually they're straight. Theatre people. You know, a few sort of up-and-coming directors and designers and stuff. You don't mind, do you?"

"Your friends are my friends, Took the Spook!" I sing.

"That's OK, then," she concludes. "It's just that I really thought it would be good for Barbara's career. Meet a few important people, but casually, socially. Know what I mean?"

I bite my tongue as the scales fall from my eyes. So that's what's going on in her scheming little mind! A cake is not enough, it seems — we've all got to spend the entire evening clearing the way for Barbara's inexorable sweep to fame!

"No problem," I mutter, going back to my beansprouts.

"Thanks, Len, you're a pal." And she bounces out.

After she has gone I get even crosser and consider cancelling the party. Up-and-coming theatre directors indeed! I can see it all — Lady Barbara fleecing about the place in some frowsy Harvey Nichols outfit pretending to be all shy, while Tookie scampers about working the crowd on her behalf! My blood boils.

Tookie comes back in. "Oh, Lenny?"

I manage my usual sweetness of tone: "Yes, Spooks?"

She shifts from foot to foot. "Well, I was just *thinking* . . ."

"Mm?"

"You know, about inviting these rather influential theatre directors and things . . ."

"No problem at all!"

"Thanks. But I was wondering, what with their being straight and so forth, I was just wondering whether you were planning on having male strippers and porno vids and things, or whether you were just going to go for the usual dips and celery?"

My hackles rise. Do I detect the ghastly spectre of censorship? My tone becomes a little crisp. "Actually, I hadn't decided whether to get in the stripper and the vids," I tell her calmly, "but there'll be dips and celery either way, rest assured of that."

"Oh good," she replies, fiddling with the door-handle. "Only, I just thought that maybe, seeing as I could probably get these people along, maybe it would be better if the party wasn't too, well, challenging I suppose. I hope you don't think I'm trying to take over!"

We both laugh matily.

"I'm sure nothing could be further from your mind," I laugh, inwardly grinding my teeth. "Tell you what, I'll let you know nearer the time. Although I must say I do feel that maybe some of these Oh-so-*Guardian*-reading up-and-coming types should take the rough with the smooth sometimes, don't you?"

"Oh absolutely — every time!" says the Spook. "I mean, *ultimately* they should have their noses rubbed in it — you know, if they want to think of themselves as having seen life. Lord yes! But I do so want to get Barbara the parts she so richly deserves, and it can be so difficult in the early years, don't you think?"

"It can."

"Obviously, later, when Barbara's famous, we won't have to worry," the Spook goes on. "I mean, we won't care, will we?"

"We just won't care!" I laugh.

My flatmate leaves, apparently satisfied that all is sorted to her liking. Little does she know. The truth is, I am now so cross that I have already decided that the porno-vids and the stripper are both *definitely on*, and there's not a thing she can do to stop me. Let her invite her directors and designers. I'm sure they just *love* Joe Orton. Well, they can jolly well wrap their jellies round some honest-to-goodness German Super-8s, and be thankful! I shall get in *Turks in the Wood* and *His Little Brother*. And they can stuff it right up their Arts Council grants! They can jolly well rub baby oil into Rick's bollocks, and I hope it gives them identity anxiety! That's the way I see it right now, anyway. Because I'm cross. Sorry, but I am.

A minute later I see Tookie dash out of the front door and I get right on the phone to Rick's agent. I am horrified to learn that he charges eighty quid a throw! But I am on the warpath now, and I track down a copy of *G.T.* and snaffle out a couple more phone numbers. In the end I find a guy who says he can get me a guy to do it for twenty-five quid, and I come straight out with it and say, Does that include the old baby oil bit? and he tells me his boys are *"very accommodating"*, in a tone which leads me to suspect that the old baby oil bit is by no means all you get for the money. All well and good, I think to myself. Let copulation thrive! We shall have blow-jobs in the living-room and sodomy on the stairs! Let them all go home suitably inspired for their forthcoming productions of *Uncle Vanya*! Then I ring up Kenny — where is all this energy coming from? — and ask him if he has any vids, or knows where I can get some. He says the last porno vid he saw was of a woman and an alsatian, and frankly he wouldn't recommend it, not unless you're in some extreme drug-warp, and actually not even then. In fact, especially not then. I say, Well, where am I going to find some stuff? Hasn't anyone got a copy of *Turks in the Wood* or *His Little Brother*? Kenny says he thinks that *maybe* our friend George has *Turks In the Wood* but he's not sure. He says, What about straight stuff? cos a friend at work has got a film about a woman with big tits and apparently it's a real laugh. I say, Straight stuff be damned! I want men, do you hear me? Men! OK, OK, Kenny says, no need to shout! I'll keep my ear to the ground, OK? OK, I say, but please don't forget — it's particularly important. Oh, and one other thing, I add: tell everyone who's coming to wear really sleazy clothes — you know, string vests and trousers with the bottom cut out and stuff like that. Kenny says OK, OK, I think I know what warp you're on, Len, and it shall be done.

Barbara comes in at two — obviously a woman of her word when it comes to early starts — and soon I am more or less kicked out of the sitting room so that she and Eric can drift about the room doing Noel Coward in the manner of Mr Spock and Zsa Zsa Gabor. All very funny I'm sure. Barbara has had this intolerably smug expression on her face ever since she stole the picture of Eric, which I must say has me absolutely flummoxed. I mean, this is obviously an example of human psychology — we all know that — but *what sort*? Though I have read extensively on the subject — yes, yes, *dipped* extensively, if we're being pedantic — I have never come across any case-studies remotely relevant to the nightmarish chain of events which has unfolded around our household over the past few days. Maybe the picture of Eric has for Barbara the valency of some sort of fetish, as if she had stolen a lock of his hair or something. Is that the word? Fetish? Maybe she fondly imagines she can possess his soul if she possesses his image. Remind me to go to the library on that one. Luckily for us all, of course, Eric's juices cannot be made to flow by members of the female sex. One assumes that Barbara is aware of this.

I drift up to Mice's room and see if he is in. He is! Enormous relief. I invite myself in for tea and we have great fun looking over some absolutely outrageous sketches he's done of his summer collection for next year. He's still very much at the men-should-wear-dresses stage, which personally I think is fine when you're young and idealistic, I mean, if I were a fashion designer I'd probably think that too. But of course the idea is patently absurd, especially in High Street terms. I grunt very politely when he shows me these particular sketches, and save my more fulsome praise for the ones of the girlies. Then we have a quick toke and I ask him if he's ever read *Blinded by the Light*. It is important for me to know the spiritual state of my flatmates. He says he hasn't, so I say, Lord! you just *have* to read this book — it'll change your life! Then I harangue him for what only seems like five minutes but is probably more like an hour about *Blinded by the Light* and he says, "Yes, Lenny, I must definitely have a gander at that book, it sounds like a hot read and no mistake."

"I didn't explain the mirrors in space very well, but you've really got to read it in context," I tell him. "It all sort of makes sense in the book. And also there's a chapter at the end which helps you to find out how many previous lives you've had, which is extremely useful to know, of course."

I go to work and we have a dress rehearsal for the cabaret. I try to watch as much of the other acts as I can because I am keen to see Bibi in a G-string, but we all have to get on with our normal cleaning duties on top of the thing, so I miss a couple of turns. Still, I am a little worried. Bibi seemed to be in the kitchen for most of the time, wearing his normal chef's outfit. If he is *not in* the cabaret I shall simply — well, I don't know what I'll do.

TWENTY-FOUR

Party-day dawns, and Kenny — thank heavens! — comes round in the morning just after lunch with a bag full of vids for me to choose from. We have a gander at a French thing with two really lovely guys in it. They're sort of hanging out on this nice farm in the countryside wearing big billowy white shirts and half-heartedly feeding the chickens and stuff, and then they go into this big old barn and get down to business. There's this voiceover blabbing on in French all the way through, and I ask Kenny what it all means.

Kenny listens and then says, "I think the voiceover is a sort of philosophical commentary on the whole thing to make it classier. It's saying, *My God! My God! Why have you created us so foul, so perverse, so degenerate?*"

"Why's it saying that?" I ask, astonished.

"I think the text is from some high-class same-sexer book from the first half of the century," says he. "They tended to go on like that in those days."

"Well, I'm not sure how much that will contribute to the party spirit," I reflect. "Religion *and* self-oppression at the same time!"

"We could just turn the sound down," says Kenny. "And anyway, no one understands French except for me. I must say I think it's bit of a winner actually. I mean, the guy on the left is a complete god, don't you think?"

I rootle through the bag a bit more. Kenny has slipped in some straight stuff, hoping I won't notice.

"What's this?" I sniff. "*Bouncing Betty Goes to Hollywood?*"

Kenny back-tracks. "Oh — I, er, knew you wouldn't want it. It just happened to be in my porno-bag."

"Well, just as long as you don't sneakily whop it on in the middle of my husband-finding," I tell him. The poor boy is into girlies as well, you see, and is constantly trying to convert his friends to his shameful perversion.

"OK," says he, a little crestfallen. "Though, in its defence, I feel bound to point out that it is actually a very witty and *up* movie, full of laughs and knowing little references to the classics of the *noir* years."

"A likely story," I snap. Then I find *Turks in the Wood, His Little Brother* and — long time no see! — a battered old copy of our friend Wieland's surrealist video classic *Chez Nous*, in which they have sex in the living room during a bourgeois cocktail party and everyone pretends not to notice. I perk up considerably when all these treasures come spilling out, and it looks as if the success of the party is assured. All I need to do now is make sure there is plenty of celery and taramasalata.

"I also brought you some trousers with the bottom cut out," says Ken, pulling out a very strange-looking garment. "I don't know if they're your size."

I am a little startled at this. "Actually, I wasn't intending to wear no-bottom trousers *myself*" I start; "I was sort of rather hoping maybe some of my guests would."

"Charming!" cries he. "You're happy for your guests to degrade themselves for your amusement, so long as *your* bottom is fully protected."

I sigh quietly. How on earth did I get myself into this? "OK," I concede, "I'll try them on. But you'll have to wait outside."

"OK, I'll go down and make us some coffee," he chirps. "And remember: no underpants. They look ridiculous with underpants."

"Can I wear a jock-strap?"

"Well, you can, but it's probably better without."

I try on the no-bottom trousers. They are made of shiny black leather. I look, of course, very strange. I look like someone wearing no-bottom trousers. You can see my bottom. I think the idea of this garment is that women have been forced to expose large expanses of their breasts over the years, so it is now high time that men showed a bit of cleavage themselves. *Mad Max II*, of course, was the occasion of the no-bottom trousers' very challenging debut in mainstream culture, and they have been a force to be reckoned with ever since, occasionally going underground but always popping up again before too long. One day they will be absolutely standard evening-wear, like the backless dress, and we will all have the pleasure of seeing Tom Cruise and Christian Slater sharing their bottoms with the rest of the world. That's the theory, anyway. I saunter about my room in the no-bottom trousers trying to forget that I am wearing them, but it's hard, very hard. I try to imagine myself straying over to the nibbles table to select myself a celery stick, you know, all casually, as one does at parties, but somehow I can't imagine myself doing it with my bottom showing. I sigh. No. It won't do. This is definitely a case of *hope one of the guests does it*, because I for one certainly haven't got the nerve. I mean, it takes all kinds to make a world. I'm sure some people could wear them without batting an eyelid. And they *do* so help a party to get off the ground.

I put my jeans back on and explain to Kenny that the trousers weren't a very good fit, though they were super-fab and I very much hope someone else will whop them on. An evil little voice at the back of my mind suggests that maybe Barney might be our man, but I am ashamed of myself for even having thought it.

Kenny goes and I troll down to the shops to stock up on celery and plastic cups. Then I spend a happy couple of hours trying on every single item of clothing I have and deciding that I look equally ridiculous in them all. I consider saying Fuck it and wearing the no-bottom trousers after all, but luckily I don't have the nerve. Eric very kindly allows his fab sound system to be requisitioned, and we carry the whole thing downstairs and set it up in the sitting-room. Everything is in readiness. I am beside myself with excitement. Before the night is through I shall be tucked up in bed with the handsomest husband a boy could possibly want!

Well, the party sort of goes OK I suppose. The main problem is I don't seem to know anyone there. They all seem to be friends of Tookie's. Mice is there, and Eric and Kenny of course, and Greg and Bjorn too. Plan C, believe it or not, runs without a hitch, and soon the American and the Swede are contentedly discussing consumer products while gazing into each other's eyes. There must be something in the air! Kenny and I run all the porno vids, but no one sees them because everyone huddles in the dining room, where you can't see the telly. It is not altogether clear as to whether or not the vids are the *cause* of everyone huddling in the dining room; on the whole I think not — it's just the way the party turns out. Luckily, the stripper doesn't show. Somehow I don't think it would have worked.

Eric gets drunk. Drunk! Eric never gets drunk! I think this must be the first time I have ever seen the boy out of his head on alcohol alone. It's usually the wicked weed that gets to him, washed down with a can of Red Stripe perhaps. But there it is: slurry words, loss of balance, the old tired-and-emotional routine. We go out into the garden. It is still pretty warm for winter. There are candles burning outside and all in all the vibe is not unmellow. For a long while Eric seems to be on the brink of spitting something out, so I hold my peace and just let him get round to it. In the end he turns to me and says, very deliberately and with a heroic attempt at a semblance of sobriety, "Lenny . . ."

"Yes, Eric?" I answer. Inside I can hear Tookie working the party: "Well, I can't really talk because she's here, of course, but it's sort of widely accepted in the business that Barbara is very soon going to be very famous indeed . . . yes . . ."

Eric sways a little and sips on his lager. Then he tells me what is on his mind. "I think . . ." he says, "I think Corey has delighted me long enough."

Big surprise. Did I hear right? Obviously the heavens and the planets and the vibes are up to some strange shit tonight! But I keep my cool and nod sagely. "Really?" I reply.

Eric sways and nods. "Yes. I think so. Long enough."

Long pause.

"Is that so?" says the up-and-coming director to Tookie behind us. "Well, I must say she is absolutely stunning to look at. Can she act?"

"Can she *act* . . . ?" says Tookie.

I try to think of something to say to Eric. In the end I settle for, "Lovely boy, Corey."

"Divine," says Eric, sipping on his lager. "Quite delightful."

And that is the last that is said on the matter.

I go back into the party and wander aimlessly through the seething crowd of straight theatre directors. My husband-finding hasn't exactly come up trumps, although I have achieved the considerable *coup* of getting rid of Greg. The thought evokes a short, cynical laugh. Some achievement! I certainly seem to be pretty good at saying no. What's wrong with me anyway? Am I doomed? Isn't there anyone out there who wants a spring lamb?

I go into the sitting-room and settle down in front of the TV. *His Little Brother* is running. Mistake. Hard realities up there on the screen. I see very clearly now that the only person to have been challenged by this party is me. I laugh again — this time letting out a harsh bray of derision directed equally at my absurd self and the world which so rashly gave me birth. If anyone heard, they probably think I have gone mad. If anyone cares, that is.

I look through to the dining room and watch all the people having a lovely time at Barbara's party. Barbara is talking to Eric. Soon the lights are all turned off and the cake is brought in. Everyone claps and sings,

Happy Birthday to you
Happy Birthday to you
Happy Birthday dear Barbara
Happy Birthday to you!

Barbara blows out the candles and they turn the lights on again. Then they all say, Make a wish, Barbara! Don't forget to make a wish! Barbara picks up the cake-knife and smiles her coy Little Miss Muffet smile and giggles something about not knowing what to wish for. One would think from the way she says it that she is vacillating between a food processor and a willowy Laura Ashley flower-print nightie. But I know better. I suddenly realize that I know better. I know exactly what Barbara is wishing for as she cuts the cake. I hear her thoughts as clear as day, ringing out across the room like spoken words:

I wish . . . I wish . . . to get inside Eric's pants!

As she cuts the cake, she looks up and sees me, through the crowd, sitting in the sitting room on my own, in the dark, my face lit by the flickering light of the TV. She smiles a little girlie smile at me, treacle and sugar and foul deception baked into a cake all its own. I try to smile back but my face is frozen into a rictus grin of loathing. She knows that I know. I know she wants Eric. *She wants Eric!*

And then — as in a theatre, when the backdrop flies up on soundless pulleys to reveal a whole new painted panorama behind, and we are transported once more, transported from fantasy to a fantasy beyond — I realize something else with blinding clarity. I realize that there is only one person who must have Eric, and that person is me!

TWENTY-FIVE

Eric is kissing Barbara . . . ! They've got their mouths open! I'm sure of it! This is . . . I thought . . .

I walk round the party very fast. Surely everyone has noticed! Surely everyone must be watching! This is the most embarrassing thing that has ever happened to me in my entire life! Why doesn't someone tell Barbara she's making a terrible mistake . . . ? warn her . . . ?

The bathroom is occupied, so I fly out of the front door and take a brisk walk round the block. It is a bit cooler outside and the effect is somewhat calming. I get back to our front door and wonder what to do. I can't go in. I just can't go in.

This is ridiculous. I live here!

I go in. Eric is still kissing Barbara. My ears explode into white-hot fountains of lava. I manage to get into the bathroom and wash my face. Then I go upstairs and go to bed. The party has delighted me long enough. I stuff bits of paper handkerchieves into my ears and wrap my head up in a pillow. Luckily I am quite drunk, and drift off into a fitful sleep.

I wake up screaming.

It is tomorrow.

Not only is it the day after yesterday but also it is *the day of the*

Christmas cabaret! I writhe about on my gritty bed-linen, moaning wordless expressions of horror. O where will my misfortunes end?

It is two o'clock in the afternoon, and we have to be in early to do the cleaning and stuff before checking our frocks and so forth. I have to get up.

I consider ringing in and saying I have a toothache but deep down inside I know I have to take my medicine. Fixing my mind on a beatific vision of Bibi in a G-string — a vision which seems to be in danger of remaining in the realms of fantasy, rather than bursting out into the real world like some all-conquering tidal wave (as once so trustingly expected) — I haul myself up from my bed. The prospect of going downstairs and facing the wreckage of Barbara's party is almost more than I can bear. Presumably I will be expected to clear it all up.

I go into the kitchen and luckily there is orange juice in the fridge, left over from last night. I make coffee. I try not to look to left or right for the first ten minutes I am in the kitchen. I am feeling a little fragile, you see.

The coffee works like a dream, and soon I am merrily going about my duties clearing up after Barbara's party. The horrors of the night before suddenly seem petty and insignificant. So what if Barbara kissed Eric? He was probably just being polite. I know that happened to me once. A girlie (actually pretty fab) said she didn't mind I was a same-sexer and just wanted a little cuddle. And then suddenly her tongue was halfway down my throat, ravishing my tonsils like there was no tomorrow! I was of course far too polite to pull away at this delicate stage. I mean, you can't, really, can you, without causing terrible upset? So anyway, that's probably what happened to Eric. Then I suddenly remember the other thing that happened last night. The other things. Corey has delighted Eric long enough! *And what else?* I rub my face and try to concentrate.

At work, Patricia and Kate and Anthea are in high spirits. Not only was *Roman Holiday* on telly last night, with Audrey Hepburn and Greg Peck both looking quite to-die-for, but also, they've been looking forward to the opportunity of prancing about onstage in ladies' clothing *all year*. I really can't understand why I am being cattle-prodded into it when there are three other members of staff, any one of which would be only too pleased to do my number for me. I look at the bookings-book and realize with a sinking feeling that the restaurant is going to be jam-packed. The Christmas cabaret, it seems, is something of a draw.

Things are real complicated. The system is that no one gets the night off tonight, so technically we are over-staffed, but everyone has to break off at some stage during the evening, change and then leap onto an extremely makeshift stage (about the size of a hat-box) while the lights are dimmed and some appalling old show-tune strikes up on the house sound-system. And then after your turn you have to *stay in drag* for the rest of the evening while you go about your "normal" waiting duties, which of course are quite soul-destroying enough when you're *not* wearing high-heels and some silly garment that is nipped in tightly at the knees. On this one night in the year we are allowed to go through to Patrick's flat, which is connected to the restaurant via a door at the back. Normally we change on the stairs before the customers arrive, and anyone who wants to make themselves look even more ridiculous than normal with make-up is free to use the loos; but tonight of course the customers are all here so we can't.

I spend the evening in a black mood, knowing that at eleven-thirty the last nail will be hammered into the coffin of my dignity. Anthea is first on at half-past-nine, and makes a complete idiot of himself as (surprise surprise) Liza Minelli. The straight French dishwasher has managed to talk himself into the G-string category and delights us at ten. Then it's Patricia. We get to eleven and I'm sort of hoping that maybe it's high time Bibi was up there revealing almost all, but instead all we get is Kate, looking quite grotesque in what was once no doubt an impenetrable Shirley Bassey disguise, but which has evidently suffered continental drift over the years and now looks more like some Voodoo devil. Maybe Bibi and the Japanese chef will do some sort of beefcake double-act later. If not, then why the hell am I here? Why am I in Patrick's bathroom being made-up by the simpering costume-master and helped into my light-up-like-a-Christmas-tree frock? Why indeed.

It's eleven-thirty, and here I am on what is passing for a stage under the intolerable scrutiny of fifty drunken punters whom I despise. My backing-track strikes up jauntily. It is the worst song in the whole world. Heaven knows where they dug it up. Presumably it's some foul old relic from the late forties, in which we are led to believe (our history, brothers!) that all-male revues enjoyed widespread mainstream popularity. Tell me about it.

I'm one of the girls
Who's one of the boys, I sing,
Enjoying the beers,
The smokes and the noise . . .

It sure feels great to be at the very forefront of Gay Lib, I must say! Nice to know one is at culture's cutting edge! We get to the second verse and Patrick flicks the switch on the power-point into which my dress is plugged. I light up like a Christmas tree.

I'm one of the queens
Who's one of the drones . . .

The punters all seem most impressed and applaud enthusiastically. The point, however, is very much lost on me.

I spend the rest of the evening in drag, serving the punters with what verges, at times, on open hostility. Calm yourself, Carnegie! Count to ten. It'll all be worth it when Bibi models that G-string.

The clock strikes twelve-thirty. I go into the kitchen pretending to get ice and casually ask Bibi when he's performing.

"You think I'm getting up on that hat-box in a G-string?" he laughs. "You must be joking!"

My world collapses about me. "I thought we ... all had to ..." I mutter.

"I told Patrick I'd hand in my notice rather than let those lousy punters drool over my pert ass," says Bibi with a cheerful grin. "That shut him up!"

When the last customers have gone there is a staff party at Patrick's place. The humiliations of the past days have so broken my spirit that, when Patrick pats me on the bum and tells me to keep my dress on I have no energy left to fight. I can't even be bothered to wash my face or change. The other waiters, of course, are all scampering about the place like new-born gazelles, beside themselves with pleasure at having an excuse to play at being girlies for the duration of a soirée. Who gives a fuck anyway? Patrick can have me for all I care. At least it'll mean *someone* wants me, which is presumably more than you can say for (for example) Patrick. I realize now that the whole thing has been entirely my own fault. I have been tricked into disgrace by my own lascivious fantasies, and I have only myself to blame. I have been hornswoggled by my hormones. O whither hast thou led me, Morocco?

Morocco, as it happens, is looking lovelier than ever tonight. He is standing with his back towards me by a table of nibbles, picking at a dish of raw vegetables. I wish he hadn't mentioned his pert ass in so many words earlier on, because it has rather drawn my attention towards that part of his adored anatomy, hugged and caressed this evening by a pair of crisp new white Levis. His hips are indeed very pleasantly narrow, and there is something quite unusually satisfying about the curvy juttingness of that posterior part which men have given a thousand names, each as inadequate as the last. Damn! I sigh a melancholy little sigh and reflect to myself that there are simply some flies in life that one will never get to unbutton. And no amount of fretting or stamping of the feet can alter that, any more than King Canute was able to turn back the tide, or Mark Anthony the clock! Ah, life! Ah, love! Ah, *lust*!

Beyond dishonour now, I mosey across the room on my gold high-heels and join Bibi at the nibbles table, opening the bidding with some fatuous remark about the importance of raw food in a balanced diet. Balanced diet indeed! What about raw meat? But — peace! Peace! Be still, my raging passions! Bibi gives me a very nice smile and says, How true, how true, all this fancy food is all very fine, but what does a body need beyond a handful of nuts and a pocketful of raisins? Why is it that Bibi and I get on so well? If only he hated me, it would be easier.

"You look good as a girl," he remarks, with a sly grin.

"Fuck that," I reply frankly, enjoying a piece of cauliflower. Then I lower my voice. "I must say I have found the whole evening a complete nightmare. This place is driving me mad."

Bibi looks around the room and mutters back, "Me too." There is a delightful hint of conspiracy in the air. "Tell you what," he goes on, "why don't we nick some beers and go up to my room and listen to some records? You like Bruce Springsteen?"

I can't stand Bruce Springsteen. "What — the Boss?" I chirp;

" — love him!" and we slip quietly out of the party.

Bibi's room is very small but it is a welcome relief from the roomful of braying transsexuals. I kind of like the way he's done it up, too — hardly any furniture, a couple of books, a couple of small souvenirs of home on the mantelpiece. Snapshots. His mum and dad. His girlfriend. His buddy from school. I get an unexpected rush of I don't exactly know what from all this intimacy — from getting so close I suppose. So close and yet so far! We crack some beers and have a great time bitching about work. Doesn't living with Patrick drive him mad? I ask. Bibi laughs and says he doesn't really care. As long as the old vampire keeps his greedy hands off Bibi's ladies-only private parts he's not too bothered. I am speechless with admiration. What serene karma the boy has! I laugh and say, I wish I felt like that about my flatmates! They drive me up the wall! He says, Why, what's been going on? I consider telling him about Barbara and Eric and everything but decide it might all sound rather sordid so I firmly draw a veil over the subject.

"I don't want to discuss my bleeding flatmates!" I announce. "I want another beer!"

We have another beer.

Then Bibi gives me another conspiratorial look. "You like ... *hashish?*" he hisses.

I throw up my hands. "Does a bear shit in the woods?" I cry. And we have a good laugh. Bibi reaches down into the bedside cupboard and brings out a hubble-bubble which looks like a family heirloom and a beautiful little hash-box with handcrafted silver decorations on the lid. The hash turns out to be the real thing and soon we are really rocking. Bibi has put lemon juice in the hubble-bubble and after we've smoked the hash we pour out the juice and make whiskey sours. Holy shit! We leave for the moon in 'zackly three minutes!

We get the giggles.

"You look so funny!" says Bibi, all red in the face, grinning from ear to ear.

"Oh shit!" I sigh. I have completely forgotten that I am still in drag. "I want to go and change ..."

I make to leave.

"Come on!" says he. "Relax! Who gives a shit? You wanna go

out there into the party and have to talk to all those morons? You're too stoned, you'd never make it down the stairs."

We both laugh. I sit down again.

"And besides, I think you look good," he adds, straight-faced. "You really look like a girl."

"I don't want to look like a girl," I pout.

"If you were a girl I'd ask you to marry me," he teases.

"You have a girlfriend," I remind him.

"Yes, but she's in Morocco."

Laughter. Pause.

Suspicion.

Frantic search of the old memory-banks through a thick haze of the old marijuana. *What is it they say about Mediterranean men?* The old memory banks whir and click, cough and splutter.

Giggle from Bibi.

Realization.

Oh my God . . .

I stand up and walk aimlessly about the room as adrenalin floods my system.

Bibi stands. "Another whiskey sour?"

"Um . . . no . . . um . . . yes . . ."

The idea of taking to my three-inch heels presents itself. I waver.

My host gives me the drink, and then bows very courteously. "Excuse me, madam," he says, "but are you free for this dance?"

"Cut it out!" I laugh, in what is intended as a very macho voice but no doubt sounds like a small furry you-know-what.

Bibi snorts with laughter. "It's just that I've been watching you sitting by yourself all evening, and as far as I'm concerned you're the prettiest girl at the party . . ."

"I'm not a girl," I reply, refusing to play ball.

He pulls me gently against his body and dances, slow and sexy. "Yes you are," he croons into my ear. "You're a girl, you're a girl, the cutest little girl I ever did see . . ."

My ears explode. My mouth goes dry. This is both intolerable and devoutly to be wished. *What the hell is going on?*

Bibi is grinding himself against me, hands on my butt. His sweet spicy breath is on my neck. Somehow we seem to have been warped into hand-shandy land — but how, and when precisely did we leave the usual three dimensions? My hands hang limply down at my side. It seems that all I have to do is accept that, for the purposes of the immediate future, I am a girl, and the doors to paradise will swing radiantly open on their golden hinges to the sound of a zillion mandolins . . . If I was a girl, I could put my hands on his back, his . . .

"I'm not a girl," I mutter.

"Yes you are," he husks.

Damn! Damn! Damn! I don't know what to do.

Haven't I been humiliated enough? Well, haven't I? But then, you do only live once (fuck *Blinded by the Light*!). How will I feel for the rest of my life if I pass up an opportunity like this? What does it matter that I'm in drag? It's just paint, just cloth, isn't it? Does a man offered caviar quibble about the cutlery?

My hands seem to have made the decision for me. They are enjoying the pleasing firmness of his denim-clad thighs . . . the glowing heat of the inside leg . . . Too late to turn back now. "OK, then" I concede at last. "Let's say I'm a girl . . . ."

"I knew you were," he chuckles, disengaging himself from me and taking a step back. Then he raises one eyebrow and says, in a very polite little voice, "Mind if I fuck your brains out?"

I am slightly scandalized by the directness of the question. "Um . . . no," I stammer, amazing myself at my ability to reply at all. Lord, how frank we are getting all of a sudden! Bibi takes all his clothes off and pushes me onto the bed. From here on the pace quickens somewhat. My dress is hitched up and my underpants unceremoniously removed. Hard realities indeed. I admire my ravisher, and wonder whether, as a girl, I am allowed and/or expected to blow him. I don't get the chance. He reaches into his bedside-drawer and takes out a tube of KY, which he expertly applies to the two points on our respective anatomies where love's friction is about to be welcomed. I have just enough time to ponder on the fact that *he has evidently done this before*, and then suddenly the time for pondering is past.

And for a while we are joined.

Bibi arrives in the Promised Land, shudders, then returns to Fulham and lights a cigarette. It becomes apparent that he does not believe in the female orgasm. I readjust my dress, as they say.

"Strong hash, huh?" quips Morocco, in what I can only assume to be intended as the ringing, clear tones of red-blooded heterosexual man-talk.

"Strong enough," I reply, disoriented.

"We've sure behaved like a couple of faggots tonight, haven't we?" he observes.

"No denying it," say I.

A little pause. Then, as if to make sure I have not missed the point, he adds, "I hate faggots, don't you?"

I am so taken aback that for a moment I am at a loss for a reply.

"Oh . . . terrible things," I mutter eventually. "Drive me mad . . ."

A moment later I realize I have just betrayed, in one fell craven swoop, my identity, my beliefs and most of my friends. I get up and go to the bathroom.

As I feverishly return my face to its rightful gender-status I go over what has just occurred and tell myself that maybe things are not as bad as they could have been. I have just allowed a man who hates faggots unprotected access to my most private part. But then — my god! I could have asked him when our next date was, if he hadn't come thundering in with his man-talk quite so promptly — if, indeed, he had left more than fifteen seconds between depositing his essences in my wombless bowels and resuming the more respected if not more traditional role of procreator. Count your blessings and make a timely exit, Carnegie me old son! The moment could have been a lot stickier.

I come out of the bathroom and pause outside Bibi's room, wondering whether or not to say good-bye. Then I think, Fuck him! and go back through the party (where I bite back a shrill cry of: Bye-bye Patrick, thanks for the party, guess whose pants I just got into?) and into the darkened restaurant. I find my clothes and change. I screw the dress up into a little ball and throw it onto the floor. Then I sit down at one of the tables and have a little cry. Get it all out of my system. Fuck them. Fuck them all. Indeed.

It's late and I wait a long time for a nightbus. The walk home from the bus-stop seems like ten miles. I get home and go upstairs. I go to Eric's room to see if there is a light on. I hear voices inside. I am about to knock on the door, when I realize that one of the voices is Barbara's. I stand outside the door for I don't know how long, then turn and go to my room.

Somehow my room seems too small, so I go downstairs into the kitchen. I look in the fridge but all the left-over taramasalata I bought for the party has been eaten. I find some celery and make some camomile tea. I go into the sitting room. I realize I am still stoned and the light is hurting my eyes. I find a candle and light it, then turn off the main light. I sit down and eat the celery and drink the tea and look at the candle. I decide that I probably won't be going back to work at Van Rijn's now. So much for pocket-money for the Christmas season. So much for buying handsome men drinks.

Footsteps on the stairs. Face peeps round the door. Little crooning voice pronounces my name: "Hi Lenny!" It is an angel from heaven. It is Barbara Honigsbaum, stoned out of her tree.

"Hi."

She looks at the candle. "Mellow vibe, huh?"

"I guess."

She comes in. Her eyes are narrowed into slits and she staggers slightly as she walks. I notice that she is wearing nothing but one of Eric's shirts. Triumph oozes from every pore.

I feel sick.

I hate her.

"Eric and I have been getting absolutely blitzed on the remains of your Leb," she confides. "I hope that's OK. Eric said you wouldn't mind."

"My Leb is your Leb," I mutter, as if reciting the Lord's prayer.

"That's OK, then," says she. "Must say it's given me a most amazing fit of the munchies, though. Think I'll go and raid the fridge!"

"Be our guest. But I don't think you'll find anything."

She goes into the kitchen and I hear her rootling about in the fridge and the cupboards. Then she comes back. In her hand is the tupperware pot. The pot of hazelnuts. She takes the lid off and peers in, straining her eyes in the flickering candlelight.

"What's in here?" she asks.

"Hazelnuts."
"Mind if I have some?"
"Go ahead."
She sits down in an easy chair.
I watch, fascinated, as she slowly eats her way through the entire contents of the pot.

TWENTY-SIX

I get up the next morning and attempt to pack all my belongings into two suitcases but somehow they don't fit. Quite apart from anything else, there's my stereo and all my records. I decide I don't care.

I stuff in the bare essentials followed by my favourite Wolfy compilations, take a last look around my room, and leave. Then I take the tube to Waterloo. At Waterloo I buy a ticket to my home town. I have to wait for twenty minutes so I mosey around WHSmiths. I buy a copy of the *New Statesman*. I get on my train.

My parents are somewhat surprised to see me, pointing out, amid twitchy smiles, that it's been four years and I haven't replied to any of their letters. They look old. Presumably I look like the whore of Babylon or something, but I am too demoralized to care.

"I saw Barney," I tell them. "He told me you were well. Can I stay for a bit?"

They say of course I can, I can stay as long as I like, etc., etc., etc., and my mum goes and puts the kettle on. It occurs to me that there are Biblical precedents for the scene we are playing out, and that probably explains why they are taking it so comparatively well in their stride.

I am surprised to learn that both my brother and my sister are now married with babies. They are twenty-one and nineteen. Obviously it is my fault for having thrown away most of my father's letters without reading them, but that doesn't stop me from being somewhat flabbergasted. One side-effect of all this fervent breeding is that there's plenty of room in the house. Johnnie and Kathy have homes of their own now, very nearby — no probs on that score.

My mum and dad and I seem to have loads to say to each other for about half an hour. My mum has discovered the raw food diet and we have fun exchanging recipes for imaginative salads. Then the stream sort of dries up. I go up to my room and unpack. I lie on my bed for a while, but the room seems funny so I walk down to the shops. There's a new estate but the old corner shop is still there. Sugar mice and sherbet fountains! Indeed. I walk down to the sea.

After supper my dad comes to talk to me in my room. He wants me to pray with him, and ask the forgiveness of both Father God and Christ Jesus (we don't care what the Holy Spirit thinks — never have) for all the sins I am assumed to have committed. He suggests that I ask Father God and Christ Jesus back into my life. It occurs to me to lay my cards on the table and point out that what I really want is the love of real 3-D people who bleed if you prick them, but no, the fight has gone out of me. It went out of me last night in an upstairs room in Patrick's flat. I'm not sure if it'll ever come back. I sit on the edge of my bed staring sulkily at the floor. "How about it?" says my Dad. I grunt and shake my head. "Maybe we can try again tomorrow," he concludes, and leaves.

Next day I decide to cheer myself up with some Christmas shopping. I go into the town centre and wander round all the tinsel displays. This for Mum. That for Dad. Johnnie. Kath. Heaven knows what you get babies for Christmas. In the shopping mall young people are standing round in groups laughing and looking kind of ugly. There's a life-size nativity scene with carols playing on a CD. Sheep. Rabbits. God. I go home. At supper we discuss my plans. I suggest that I might pick up the threads of my librarian career in the new year, and if it takes off, start to look for a flat of my own soon after. Everyone thinks this is a splendid idea. After supper I have to fend off my evangelizing father yet again, then I take an early night. I have no energy.

I dream that I'm a shepherd. I live in the Middle East, only it's much greener than the Middle East you see on telly, it's really quite nice. Eric is a shepherd too and I'm his boyfriend. Life is simple but never dull.

Then an angel comes down and tells us there's this really wild happening on the cards in Bethlehem, and we should drop what we're doing and hot-foot it over there if we know what's good for us. This sort of guru has been born, and he radiates good vibes, enough in fact to transform the whole tired old world into a buzzing love-in. Eric and I rush to Bethlehem and sure enough there's this stable with lots of light flooding out of it! We go in. There are sheep and rabbits and squirrels and chipmunks and mice and horses and cows, all standing round the manger singing carols and stuff. We explain that we're poor and we haven't brought a present, but we just wanted to pay our respects, I mean, how could we not?

Suddenly the baby jumps up in the manger and points at me and Eric and starts shouting about how we're wicked and unclean and have no right to be there at all, and all the chipmunks and squirrels look at us, appalled. Hideous embarrassment. Then the baby turns into a sort of dwarf-version of Bibi, and jumps up and down in the manger screaming obscenities at us and calling us faggots. A chipmunk tactfully takes me to one side and whispers in my ear that maybe it might be better if we just quietly left. I wake up sweating.

The next night I have a dream that I am personally crucifying Christ Jesus. Excruciating guilt. I'm right there, on top of the poor man, hammering those nails in like they were cricket-stumps or something. Then he looks at me and I stop.

"Lenny," he says.

"Yes," I mutter.

"Why are you crucifying me?"

"Um . . . I don't know," I reply.

He gives me a rather withering look and says, "Why can't you be nice?"

"Um . . . I don't know," I tell him. "I would be if I knew how. What should I do?"

"Give up boys," he tells me. "Give up drugs. Stop believing in reincarnation. Go to church."

"Sounds simple enough," I concede.

"It is," he says. "So just do it, OK?"

The next day I invite Christ Jesus and Father God back into my life. I feel much better. My whole being is flooded with inner light. I tell my mum and dad and of course they're delighted. We discuss my future some more. They tell me that I should proceed with extreme caution for the next few weeks, because the Devil will be absolutely livid about me going good, and will be trying extra hard to tempt me back onto the road to hell. I should stay at home as much as possible, and only go out accompanied. They suggest that I have no further contact with my friends from London, not even via the phone or letters. This seems a little hard but I defer to their better judgment. After all, I am on a sort of cure, and it's a bit like being on a diet really, in that you can't argue with the doctor. So I say, OK, but how am I going to get my stereo back and stuff? My Dad tells me not to worry, and he'll fix it.

A girl who works in the local hairdressers comes round and dies my hair back to its original colour (mouse). Everyone is terribly pleased with the results.

Then it's Christmas, which of course is great fun.

TWENTY-SEVEN

It's February now, and I must say I'm beginning to feel like I never went away. The library welcomed me back with open arms — obviously I have always been considered something of a star there. Well, it's certainly good to be gainfully employed. The whole idea of me getting a flat of my own has been put more or less permanently on ice. There really is no immediate need for me to move out. There's so much room, what with Johnnie and Kath having places of their own. I think Mum and Dad are quite glad to have somebody around, all in all.

I have two nephews, and I can report that I have taken to unclehood like a duck to water. You should see their chubby little faces light up when their Uncle Lenny comes round bearing sweeties and bags of crisps and stuff! My brother-in-law is sort of all right, and my sister-in-law (Mandy) is actually a real gem. Quite how Johnnie managed to bag her shall always be a mystery to me, she's far too good for him! Oh, the joys of family life!

I have all my own stuff back now. (Quite strange note here: Eric very kindly drove all my stuff down in Tookie's minibus, but delivered it all when I was out and didn't even leave a note saying Hi or anything. I am a little surprised that Eric hasn't written — I mean, *I* have a good reason for not writing, viz: that my dad won't let me — I'm still sort of in quarantine, as it were, because my conversion back to good is obviously pretty fresh, on the long-term scale, and this is apparently an absolutely classic time for the Devil to make his move — about six weeks after you go good — just about the time when you're beginning to relax and think you've seen the last of the old dog. Well, that's when he comes down on you like a ton of bricks. And that's why I'm not allowed to write to Eric or anyone. But I must say I can't help feeling that a friendship of four years ought to be worth at least a postcard from his end. But still. I don't really care, as obviously all that stuff is in the past now.) (Postscript to note: I'm not absolutely sure, but I have a *leetle* suspicion that the quarantine which my dad has arranged for me may extend to his not passing on phone-calls if he believes them to be from London. Well, where else would they be coming from, apart from Johnnie's or Kath's? I did once come out onto the landing and hear him saying *No, I'm afraid he isn't home* — and who else could "he" have been except me? Not that I mind — I think he's probably quite right. I think it is absolutely essential not to look back in life, on pain of being turned into a pillar of salt — don't you?)

When I look back on my time in the Big Bad City, I must say I can't help wondering, Was that wild, crazy, *sad* little person really me? Because I was sad, deep down, all along — just pretending to be happy really I think — covering it all up with getting stoned and filling my mind with lustful thoughts — and all the time it was because there was something missing from my life. I suppose I need hardly mention what that something was. If you don't know yourself — if you've never had any sort of yearning feeling in your soul for some sort of Higher Truth, for something outside of yourself which is *greater than yourself* but which takes a personal interest in your day-to-day affairs, then I don't really think anything I can say will be able to explain it to you. I'm talking about Father God and Christ Jesus here, of course. For the benefit of the determinedly unspiritual I suppose I might as well spell it out in words of less than three syllables.

"Dad," I muse, toying with my yummy dinner, "what sort of time does a spiritual quarantine usually run for?"

My dad chews thoughtfully. "Impossible to say," he at length replies. "We won't really know if it is over until we get the word from Father God or Christ Jesus."

"Oh."

"Maybe it will never be over," he adds after a pause.

"*Never?*" I am a tad surprised at this.

My dad looks at me with his kind old eyes. "You have to remember, Lenny, that you have strayed quite a long way off the straight and narrow path. A lot further off than most of us stray. You're going to have to be a lot more careful than the rest of us when it comes to watching out for old Horns-And-Curly-Tail. Right now he is grinding his teeth and jumping up and down — spitting with fury over the fact that you've gone good. He was really pretty convinced he had you, you see. You've got to try to see it from his point of view."

"I see."

"He'll always be cross about letting you slip through his fingers, and he'll always make special efforts to get you back. We're going to have to watch over you extra carefully, otherwise he might snatch you right up out of your bed. I'm speaking figuratively, of course, but you know what I mean."

I give a reflective little sigh, not untinged with melancholy. "It just seems so sad that I am never to see my old friends again," I ponder. "I mean, I know they're wicked, but they wouldn't fool me a second time, would they? Couldn't I just nip up to London for the day and put my head round the door? I wouldn't even stay the night!"

"I wouldn't be so sure they wouldn't fool you a second time," says he.

Then I have a marvellous idea. "Couldn't I try to convert them?"

My father puts down his fork. "Correct me if I'm wrong," says he, "but wasn't it your trying to convert them that was precisely where the rot set in in the first place?"

"Oh, yes," I confess. "I had forgotten about that. Oh well, no turning back I suppose."

My mum pats my hand. "That's my boy," says she.

I know, deep down, that they are right.

Sad, though, all the same.

I go back to my dinner and resign myself to permanent quarantine.

"But you can see you brother-in-Christ-Jesus Barney," says my dad. "That would be quite permissible."

I perk up a little. Barney would be better than nothing, fun though my home town is, with its marvellous shopping mall and library.

We do have a load of laughs at the library, that cannot be denied. Now that I'm back it's just like old times. Lisa and Abby are still there, a little older (but apparently none the wiser!) and they are full of stories about the various people who tried to replace me, each one failing more dismally than the last. What it boils down to is that librarianship is something that requires flair — you know — *panache* — and if you haven't got it, you're really just getting in the way.

We don't get to have our lunches at the same time, because you've always got to have at least two people "on the floor," but we try to overlap by a few minutes whenever possible in order to catch up on gossip and compare sandwiches in the back room. Lisa and Abby love to hear me talk about my time in the big city, although I am careful to select my stories sensitively. I mean, some things are better left unsaid, as the lovely old song goes. In many ways it's nice to be a big fish in a small pool. They're so easily impressed.

"Oh, Lenny," says Lisa, finishing her baguette with cottage cheese (her lunch-break is nearing its end, mine is just starting), "you are a scream! We're not really glamorous enough for you, are we?"

I stop unwrapping my baguette with cottage cheese and look up. Somewhere in the back of my mind an old bell tolls. Where did I hear that said before?

"Nonsense," I snort. "Glamour is an illusion. You wouldn't like London if you actually went there, any more than I did."

"Oh, you know what I mean," she goes on. "You're too wild and wacky for librarianship. You need something more creative."

I put my baguette carefully down on a copy of *Tristram Shandy*.

"That's absurd," I reply calmly. But deep down inside, my equilibrium has been somewhat disturbed. The ghosts of my past life, wilder than the wind, are shrieking in the windmills of my mind. *Will I never be free?*

I decide to ring the changes on my usual lunchtime routine and eat my baguette by the river instead of in the back room. Well, why not? I sit for a while looking at the dry, litter-filled channel which used to be a babbling waterway and reflect for a while upon the circular nature of existence. Then it occurs to me that it might be a sin to think of existence as circular, and so I wisely get up and buy myself a copy of *TV Times*, which I go back and enjoy in the back room for ten minutes before resuming my duties. How Jayne Seymour manages to keep her looks the way she does certainly is something of a miracle.

Abby comes in with her baguette, which she excitedly tells me has not only cottage cheese in but also some small chunks of pineapple. We both agree that this is something of a breakthrough, and resolve to be increasingly bold in our sandwich-filling experiments.

I put down my copy of *TV Times*. "Abby," I muse.

"Yes?" says she.

"I was just thinking . . ."

"Don't strain yourself!" she quips.

"No — I want to ask your advice," I tell her.

"OK. Try me."

"Well . . . I was just thinking . . . You know with diets and stuff . . ."

Abby and I are always talking about food, and she always seems to be on a diet.

"Don't tell me you're going on a diet!" she positively screams. "But you're all skin and bones!"

"No — no, it's not me," I tell her. "It's a friend. I just wanted to ask you, if you were on a diet, and it was terribly strict, and you had to be on it for a long time, would you ever, well, have just a very small cream bun or something? I mean, just every once in a while, just to make you feel better?"

Abby puts on her special I'm-the-expert voice.

"Listen," she says. "Tell your friend: *no diet is so important that you have to make your life a misery*. Tell your friend: *If you want the cream bun, have it – but only one!*"

"Do you really think so?" say I.

"I know so," says she. "You see, it's all to do with mental attitude. There's no point in replacing an obsession with food with an obsession with dieting."

I am struck — as I often am — by the wisdom of her words.

"But what if the doctor told this friend of mine that he absolutely mustn't eat any cream buns at all?" I insist.

"Oh, for heaven's sake!" says Abby. "Tell your friend that he's got to learn to be his own man. Tell him to declare his independence for once. I'm sure one little cream bun isn't going to kill him."

On my way home I stop off at a phone booth and ring Eric. Tookie answers the phone.

"I'm afraid he's not in," she chirps. "Can I take a message?"

In a way I am relieved.

"Um . . . yes," I reply. "Tell him I said thanks for bringing my stuff down."

TWENTY-EIGHT

Shortly after we have established that it is permissible for me to see Barney, my mum gets on the old blower and invites him down for an extra-scrummy Sunday lunch.

It's the first time I've met Barney's wife, and also the first time I've seen him since Eric and I so unfortunately interrupted Barney's breaking the ice with Corey. Barney says Hi and How have you been etc., etc., etc., and I can't help feeling that those big bloodhound eyes of his are sort of adding an unspoken, pleading *P.S.* It's OK, Barnes me old mucker! I mean, *would* I? What sort of fiend in humanoid form do you think I am? We all make mistakes. Far be it from me.

We go to church, and the service is very lively. There's a little group playing along with the hymns — just an acoustic guitar, drum-kit and tambourine, but it makes all the difference. Whoever said church couldn't be with-it? The big hit of the service is that very *up* one which goes:

Yes Jesus loves me
Yes Jesus loves me
Yes Jesus loves me
The Bible tells me so.

It has a terrific tune and you can really let rip in it. After church we take the scenic route for a relaxed walk home while Mum dashes back in the car to get all the food ready. Actually my home town doesn't immediately suggest the word "scenic", but the point is, we take the route that avoids the path with extra helpings of dogshit. On the way back Barney tells us the amazing news that he and his lovely wife are thinking of moving out of London. We all say, Oh Barney! Barney! Come and live here! and Barney laughs and says, Well, we'll have to think about that — we haven't even decided for sure that we're leaving. Apparently it's really Barney's wife who wants to move.

"She never did like the big city much — did you, dear?"

"I don't mind it," says his wife. "It's just that I got my handbag snatched, and after a thing like that happens, you don't really feel the same about a place."

Barney gives us a funny, knowing smile and tells us that she didn't *really* get her handbag snatched.

"Yes I did!" cries she, "In the middle of King Street!"

Barney sighs. "No you didn't," he says tolerantly.

"Yes I did!" she cries.

Barney sighs again, gives us a little smile as if his wife is some sort of nut-case, and no more is said of the matter. But I must say it does strike me as rather odd. I mean, either she had her handbag snatched or she didn't. I would have thought that it must be rather difficult to disagree on a thing like that.

We have a lovely lunch and after it we all feel very full. We play with Barney's baby. It is quite nice. I almost fall asleep from being too full, but leap up just in time and make some strong coffee. Later on Barney suggests that we go out for another walk, just him and me. I say, What a marvellous idea, Barnes me old china, and we leap out, leaving everyone else snoozing and belching in the rather over-hot house. Barney goes to open his car, and I say, I thought we were going for a walk! Barney says, Well, yes, but why don't we go for a walk somewhere nice? I always wanted to see that old fort you used to talk about. I say, OK, why not? And we drive down to the fort and park the car and stroll around the nice lawns and things. It gets dark. Barney and I are having a very mellow chat, and it seems a pity to end it, so by common consent we head for the nearest pub.

We go in.

Eric is there.

For a split-second I am under the impression that some flabbergasting coincidence has occurred, and then I realize in a blinding flash that I have in fact been *taken* to this pub by Barney, even though he made it look like the other way around. The whole thing has been set up. I waver, suspecting perhaps that this is the Devil's work, and consider walking straight out of the door again. After all, I *was* warned to be on the look-out.

Eric says Hi and gives a nice little smile and I husk out some greeting or other and wonder what the hell is going on. Barney and Eric. A most interesting combination. Barney and Eric in league in some way.

"Why didn't you write?" says Eric.

"Why didn't *you* write?" I husk.

"I did," says he.

"Oh." No use arguing the toss. Presumably the old quarantine routine extended to interception of mail. Fair enough.

"So what's life like down here?" says he.

Funny vibe.

"Super-fab," I assert, overcompensating a little. Then I add, "Thanks for bringing down my stuff."

"You're welcome."

Barney brings us some beers and then (I realize later) sort of disappears. Dissolves. Is not seen again. I stare into my beer. I look Eric in the eye. I must say I seem to be beyond pussyfooting, one way and another. "How's Barbara?" I enquire bitterly.

"Fine, I guess," says he. "*Private Lives 2000* fell through."

"Oh, I'm sorry to hear that," I lie.

"Yes, the Noel Coward estate wouldn't let us do it in sci-fi outfits. They said, tuxedos or nothing, matey!"

"Well, whatdya know?"

"Silly, huh?"

Silence. Beer.

"I hope you'll be very happy together," I bleat, sounding as tight-arsed as a ninety-year-old spinster. Then I blush, and gulp at my drink. Eric sighs and I think he probably smiles too, but I'm not sure because I'm not looking at him.

"There's nothing between Barbara and me," he says in a calm voice.

I snort. I huff. I am not very good at this sort of thing. "You certainly seemed to be on pretty matey terms when I was last in town," I point out.

"I slept with her once," says he.

My face burns. The fact that Eric only slept with Barbara once somehow doesn't seem to make it any better. In fact, hearing him wrap his tongue around the concept of sex with Barbara *at all* makes my head spin. I try to look away, but there's nowhere else to look except Eric and my beer.

He taps my hand. "Lenny . . ."

I start getting all cross. "Leave me alone."

". . . lighten up."

"Don't you tell me to lighten up," I snap.

Eric sighs and sits back. For a moment he looks round the pub and runs his hands through his hair. Then he leans forward on the table again. "How old am I?" he asks.

"What?"

"How old am I? I'm asking you."

I look at him blankly. *What new madness is this?* "I dunno," I pout.

"Well, how old do you think I am?"

I shrug. "Twenty-five? Twenty-six?"

"I'm thirty-two."

Silence. Beer. "So what?" I reply.

Eric looks at the ceiling as if for inspiration. "Don't you think I know what I want?"

"Maybe you do. Maybe you don't," I sniff. "What's it got to do with me?"

He scratches his head. "You are . . . you are just the most . . ."

"The most what?"

"I dunno . . . I give up."

We finish our beers. It's as if there's something more to say — something important. We get up to leave. We walk out into the car-park. "Where's Barney?" I ask.

"I told him I'd drive you back," says Eric.

"Oh."

Tookie's minibus is parked outside the pub. I wonder why I didn't notice it before.

"Barney set this up, didn't he?"

"He's a good guy," says Eric. "Friends are more important to him than ideas."

We get into the bus and drive off.

I realize we are driving to London. Somehow I haven't got the strength to fight it.

"I thought you were driving me home," I mutter.

"Shut up," says Eric.

Intriguing. It seems that something has changed. Or at least, is about to. Have I missed the point? Or is it becoming a different point?

The journey. Motorway, tail-lights in the dark, trees. A smidgeon of Elton crackles across the speakers. Those chords. That piano.

London.

We get back to the house. We go in. We go into the kitchen.

"Clear the kitchen table," says Eric.

"Good idea," say I. "Shall I put together a quick spaghetti or something?"

"No," says Eric. "Clear the kitchen table."

TWENTY-NINE

Barney and his wife didn't move out of London in the end. They still live just down the road from us, and we see them all the time. We feel we owe Barney so much. Well, we do. Added to which, the gulf between me and Barney has somewhat narrowed, what with one thing and another. I think the whole Corey thing narrowed it considerably — Lord, I almost forgot! there's *more to tell*! You won't believe this, but apparently (from what one can gather) Corey *fell in love with Barney*! Can you believe that? With the old bloodhound himself! And Barney said — and this was one of his better moments, I think — Barney said, Sorry, me old mucker, I was but a day-tripper to Sodom: strictly no sale! And Corey is said to have cried and pleaded and stood outside Barney's window in the pouring rain, and slept on his doorstep all night, and begged him to have him as his boyfriend, but Barney was Adam Ant. Not only am I married, says he, but also, even if I wasn't, I'm afraid I prefer girlies and that's just your hard Cheddar! One can't help laughing. Legend has it — so difficult to substantiate these things — that Barney, after several weeks of this hysteria from old Mister Sex-In-The-Bushes, finally gave him a good old talking to and told him that if he wanted any part of him he would just have to transfer all his doomed sexual energy into something more sanctified and become Barney's brother-in-Christ, and (can you believe this?) Corey says, Oh Barney, Barney, anything you say! I'd do anything just to have a little part of you! I'll give up boys! I'll give up the Heath! I'll invite not only Father God but also Christ Jesus into my life, if it will mean that you'll let me sit next to you in Church on Sundays! And Barney says, Off you go, then! Here's a Bible and a prayer-book — now run along and get saved and don't come back until you are! . . . Oh — life, life! What a strange, mad muddle!

Bjorn has moved in with Greg — thank God! — and Mice has invited his very sweet boyfriend Tony to live with us. Tony is small but perfectly formed, like a little miniature Greek statue. You want to stand him on your coffee-table. Tookie, bless her, now has a place of her own, as she's making loads of money out of Barbara, who, as it turns out, really has become famous after all. She has her own TV show. It's just called *Honigsbaum* — no frills, just *Honigsbaum* — and it has a title-sequence with Barbara attempting to do a little dance (she can't dance) while there is a little inset of her face in close-up in a corner of the screen, just smiling and laughing and being beautiful. The show is absolutely super-fab and we all love it. We watch it every week, and if we are going to be out, we always get a friend to tape it.

Now, you are probably assuming (in your clever, witty, worldly way) that, just because I decided to go back to live in London and resume my career as a practising homosexualist, I once again renounced my faith and dove back into my former state of half-baked paganism. Nothing could be further from the truth. You see, I have mellowed — like a fruit. Like a fruit that has lain in the warm sun for many a day and is contemplating turning at last to a ripe sweetness that shall bless some simple farmer's table, I have mellowed. I try now to avoid, wherever possible, those wild big swings of the pendulum which send us reeling from one extreme to the next — those see-saw heave-hos that make the soul giddy and sick. There can be no peace in such an existence, and I will have none of it, I say! No — moderation is now my middle name. Moderation and, yes, even a little smidgeon of compromise. I have made a deal with Father God and Christ Jesus. I have explained to them that I am actually perfectly happy for them to be in my life, provided they don't hog all the space and crowd out everyone and everything else, like they did before. I have discussed with them the small matter of my sleeping with Eric, and we all agree that actually it's no particularly big thing, and that if that's my way of appreciating the glory of creation, then so be it. I have pointed out to God that I think his Bible has been a little corrupted over the years, a little politicized, and he said, Yes actually you're right — it doesn't do to take it too literally. You've got to take it in the spirit it was originally intended. And so now we are the best of friends. There is a lesson here for all of us. Eric, of course, ever the serene cynic, is not above taking the piss out of my simple devotions, but I can take it, and deep down inside I harbour a lurking suspicion that one of the best methods of conversion is just quietly getting on with it and letting the infidel soak up the vibes in his own time. He'll be laughing on the other side of his face one day, you mark my words.

And so, you see, that is why Barney and I are now the best of friends. We have, as it were, met each other halfway. He has demonstrated — memorably — that he is not impervious to the temptations of the flesh, while I have conceded that I am not immune to the charms of the divine. Added to which, he will always occupy a very special place in my heart and in Eric's too, for we shall never forget that he was the person who brought us together when things were least auspicious.

What more can I say? Life goes on. We don't go out quite as much as we used to. The house is a little cleaner since Bjorn moved. Our needs are few and simple. All we really need of an evening is Eric, me, a bottle of white wine and (to quote the lovely old song) a table made of wood.

P.S.

"But you still haven't told them the story!"

"What do you mean, I still haven't told them the story?"

"What I say! You kept starting to tell them, then you'd get distracted and go rabbiting on about something completely different . . ."

I sigh in exasperation. What is Eric on about? "I must say I thought I had told the whole thing rather well," I sniff.

Eric sighs too. "The story you set out to tell in the first place. How you lost that which can never be regained," he explains.

I stop and consider. I realize with some concern that he is right. "Shit!" I hiss. "And now I've finished!"

"You'll just have to go right back to the beginning and start again," says he.

He is right. There is no getting away from it.

Back I go!

ONE

The story of how I lost that which can never be regained — my innocence — has amused many a dinner-party of bright young same-sexers in the Hammersmith and Shepherds Bush neck of the woods. My flatmate Eric says it is the most erotic story he has ever heard — which is good of him, really, considering it was his lovely boyfriend Corey who seduced me. I was going from door to door attempting to make converts for the over-lively Church to which I belonged ("Hello we're from the local church and were just wondering whether you were interested in Father God or Christ Jesus at all and whether you might like to invite them into your life at all and if not whether you might like to talk about it at all and if not *why not* and if not not NOT then is there anyone else in the house who you think *might* be interested in Father God or Christ Jesus . . . at all?") and I had split up from my brother-in-Christ Barney so that we might get the street finished quicker and thus not miss the ineffable opening of the evening's Pink Floyd gig, which, rumour had it, made your mind explode into a zillion brightly-coloured splinters.

When I first proposed conversion to Corey, who opened the door, he dismissed me peremptorily with a sleepy glare and a barked command of *Piss off*. The door slammed in my face and it started to rain. I walked out into the street and looked down the road, trying to work out how many more houses I had to do, and whether I would get them all done in time. I had no umbrella. I don't know how long I stood outside the house in which I was later to become resident — how long did it take Corey to form his fiendish plan? — but after a minute or maybe five, the door was opened once more, and I heard a voice behind me say,

"You're wet."

He was wearing a white towelling robe, sort of half-open at the chest, and I must say I thought I'd died and gone to heaven.

"Yes," I replied tremulously, like a small furry animal crying for its mother; "I forgot my umbrella."

Corey stood in the doorway for a moment, insolently watching me being rained on, then gave me a little handsome smile and confessed, "I'm sorry I snapped at you. It's just that I'm not at my best in the morning. Your job must be very wearing. Can I make it up to you by giving you a cup of tea?"

There was something about the way he said it — polite but yet just a tiny bit more intimate than normal social codes might permit — that set my heart a-pounding. I sighed with grateful relief at the prospect of tea and stepped inside.

"I declare a small dish of tea would be quite wildly comforting," I quavered, looking in astonishment around the room. A newspaper for same-sexers lay shamelessly on the coffee-table. Last night's dope and incense hung in the air.

Corey served the tea and got to the point with a swiftness the like of which I have never seen before or since.

"Listen," he said, "About this God-stuff . . ."

"Um, yes," said I, trying to sound very businesslike. "I was just wondering whether you were interested in Father God or Christ Jesus at all and whether you might—"

"Yes, yes, I know all that," he snapped. "You were wondering whether I might like to invite them into my life. Well, to be perfectly frank, I *have* considered it."

"You *have*?" I was amazed. Somehow he didn't look like the sort of person who lay awake at night worrying about eternal damnation.

Corey seated himself on the leopard-skin sofa which was in the house at the time, and the towelling dressing-gown rode up to reveal miraculous expanses of milky thigh, soft and pure, unlike my thoughts.

"Yes, I have," he drawled, sipping on his tea and looking at me as if reading my very soul with his all-too-knowing eyes. I wriggled in my seat. I looked at his legs.

"Tell you what," he piped up after a pause, "I'll make you a bet."

"A *bet*?"

"Yes, we'll toss a coin. We'll bet on my salvation."

Nothing Aunt Amber had told me about converting sinners had prepared me for this one.

"Oh," I replied. "I'm not sure—"

"Why not? Don't they encourage you be imaginative in your work? Did you never see *Guys and Dolls*?"

"Um, yes . . ." I wavered, "but—"

"But what?" said he jauntily. "I'm prepared to stake my soul against — oh, I don't know . . ."

"50p?" I suggested. I was not rich.

"50p?" he cried. "Isn't it worth more than that?"

I didn't know what to say. This was the strangest reaction I had ever got to my "Father God" speech. Could I handle it? Did I *want* to handle it? Should I flee?

"Let's say —" said Corey, " — for the sake of a few laughs — *your underwear*. My soul against your underwear. What do you think? Heads or tails?"

I lost the bet.

* * *

GMP books can be ordered from any bookshop in the UK, and from specialised bookshops overseas. If you prefer to order by mail, a comprehensive catalogue is available on request, from:

GMP Publishers Ltd (GB),
P O Box 247, London N17 9QR.

In North America order from Alyson Publications Inc.,
40 Plympton St, Boston, MA 02118, USA.

In Australia order from Bulldog Books,
P O Box 155, Broadway, NSW 2007, Australia.

Name and Address in block letters please:

Name
_____

Address
_____

_____

_____